FEAR OF
DREAMS:
THE COMMUNE

FEAR OF DREAMS:

THE COMMUNE

VICTORIA LEE

Archway Publishing books may be ordered through booksellers or by contacting:

Archway Publishing
1663 Liberty Drive
Bloomington, IN 47403
www.archwaypublishing.com
844-669-3957

Because of the dynamic nature of the Internet, any web addresses or links contained in this book may have changed since publication and may no longer be valid. The views expressed in this work are solely those of the author and do not necessarily reflect the views of the publisher, and the publisher hereby disclaims any responsibility for them.

Any people depicted in stock imagery provided by Getty Images are models, and such images are being used for illustrative purposes only. Certain stock imagery © Getty Images.

ISBN: 978-1-6657-5205-3 (sc)
ISBN: 978-1-6657-5206-0 (e)

Library of Congress Control Number: 2023920297

Print information available on the last page.

Archway Publishing rev. date: 10/24/2023

This book is lovingly dedicated to my loving husband, Doug, who has always believed in me.

CONTENTS

Chapter 1   Finding My Joy...1
Chapter 2   Waking Up with Joy...5
Chapter 3   The Calm before the Storm..............................9
Chapter 4   Life at the River Goes On............................. 15
Chapter 5   Commune Dreams 21
Chapter 6   Therapist Woes 25
Chapter 7   Commune Investigations 31
Chapter 8   The Sneakiness Continues.............................35
Chapter 9   Church Encouragement.................................39
Chapter 10   The Night Terrors Continue..........................43
Chapter 11   The End of Spencer..49
Chapter 12   Bloody Night Terrors 53
Chapter 13   Commune Scrutiny 57
Chapter 14   Caught Again 61
Chapter 15   Listening..65
Chapter 16   Missing Rachael..71
Chapter 17   Punishment Woes..75
Chapter 18   Detecting Nothing 79
Chapter 19   Out of the Box..85
Chapter 20   Brainwashing Saga..91
Chapter 21   Will It Ever Stop?...97
Chapter 22   The House of Torture 101
Chapter 23   Torturous Memories 105
Chapter 24   Back Home Investigations............................ 109
Chapter 25   Feeling Nothing... 113

Chapter 26 Probation Time.................................... 119

Chapter 27 Happy Freedom 123

Chapter 28 Secret Memories 127

Chapter 29 Walks with Cindy............................... 131

Chapter 30 Scary Movies 137

Chapter 31 Scary Things in the Dark.................... 141

Chapter 32 The Investigations Continue 147

Chapter 33 The Way to a Better Life 149

Chapter 34 A New Day.. 155

Chapter 35 Chores Begin 159

Chapter 36 Cindy and Frank................................. 163

Chapter 37 Worship Night Life............................. 167

Chapter 38 The Nightmares Continue 171

Chapter 39 Washing Windows.............................. 177

Chapter 40 Spencer's Information 183

Chapter 41 Evil Séance 185

Chapter 42 The Beat Goes On 189

Chapter 43 Love and Marriage............................. 193

Chapter 44 Wedding Day 197

Chapter 45 Moving In with Jerry.........................205

Chapter 46 Morning Sickness 211

Chapter 47 Strangers... 215

Chapter 48 Sleepless Nights................................ 219

Chapter 49 Officer Dale's Lead 223

Chapter 50 The Truth Comes Out 225

Chapter 51 And So It Begins Again 229

Chapter 52 Back to the House of Blood 233

Chapter 53 Bloody Thoughts...............................237

Chapter 54 Trips to Town 241

Chapter 55 Near Normal 245

Chapter 56 Back to the House of Peace................ 249

Chapter 57 Come Find Me 255

Chapter 58 Nightly Investigations....................... 257

Chapter 59 Nightly Rituals.................................. 261

Chapter 60 Fear Escapes Me 263
Chapter 61 Frank and Cindy Go to Town............................ 267
Chapter 62 Evil to Come... 271
Chapter 63 Helping Miranda 275
Chapter 64 Preparation 281
Chapter 65 The Rescue... 285
Chapter 66 My Gary.. 287

CHAPTER ONE
FINDING MY JOY

I'm running down to the river, holding hands with Gary. We are laughing and having so much fun. You see, Gary is the love of my life. I am so happy with him. God truly blessed me with a wonderful man. I know I will never find another Gary. He is one of a kind.

As we get closer to the water, I look toward the rocks at the shallow part of the river and see something floating on the water. We walk slowly over to that part of the river. I'm still holding Gary's hand because I'm so scared of what I will see as we approach the water. What is it, Rachael? Will it be a nightmare again where I see my friends dead. How bad it was to go to both of their funerals. Oh, my goodness, it's Ryan and Sarah swimming and having fun. I stare at them in disbelief. How can they be alive? For heaven's sake, I saw their small caskets put down in the ground that dreadful day when we were kids. When I look closer, I see they both have angel wings attached to their backs. How can this be? I see them smiling and happily splashing in the water. They look at me and then at Gary, and they blow kisses at us.

As I awake, I know this is a heavenly vision that has been sent to show me happiness and joy.

What a great dream to know that my friends are OK and happy in another world, heaven that is. I truly believe this vision was shown to me in my dream so I could have peace. My dreams are less frequent and becoming more bearable now. Some of them make me feel so peaceful at night when I wake up. However, I still need to continue attending my therapy sessions and group classes and taking my medications. I still have bad dreams, but since I started getting help, they are not as frequent or as horrendous, full of terror, causing me to scream during the night. At least I'm not dreaming about murders, knives, and dead people at this point in my life, and I'm not scaring my family. It is a good feeling that gives me hope for a better life.

I lay awake in my bed next to Gary, my one true love. He has been here for me since the horrible events that happened in my life over the past couple of years. He was there for the murders I witnessed at our beloved river, my runaway flight for life, and my rescue. I could not believe things turned out well for me and that I'm still alive. I got my husband, Gary, my two beautiful boys, and my family back. How fortunate for me that God blessed me during these horrible events that occurred in my life. I got myself into horrible things.

I'm thinking about the whole scenario I was involved in. When I was a kid, I witnessed horrible killings at the river. Harold was a weird kid who swam with us. I once saw him kill a cat down the road from his house. Growing up, I stayed away from him because he knew I had witnessed him killing my friends Ryan and Sarah. As an adult, I went to a dreadful dinner for Gary's school board at Harold's

house. I knew he was going to kill me—and his father, Johnny—
that night. I escaped and got a ride with a girl named Cindy. She
took me to a religious commune, which ended up involving church,
weddings, chores, rape, beatings, and murder.

I got married again at the commune, to a man named Jerry.
What was I thinking being married already and then marrying another guy? I stabbed Cindy and Jerry because I caught them together
in my bed. But maybe that was just one of my dreadful dreams.
There was no evidence of my bloody dress, the knife, or anything
reported about a double homicide in the news. I escaped by stealing
Cindy's car. I returned home to Mama and Dad.

I watched Harold's house at night from my hiding place, leaving
special packages with notes. I'm not sure how I found the courage
to go out at night and sneak around. Even though I was so scared
of Harold, I wanted him to know I was back in town. He needed
to know I was coming for him. I knew I needed to kill him before
he murdered me like he murdered my friends. I saw Harold killing
himself at the river as his father watched. He repeatedly stabbed
himself in the stomach. There was blood everywhere. As Johnny
walked away, I saw Harold floating in a pool of blood. It looked like
red smoke dissolving in the water. Oh, the things I got myself into.

After Harold was dead, I knew Johnny was still out there, and
he was possibly coming for me. He probably knew I witnessed the
children's murders a long time ago and saw Harold committing sui-
cide. What else was Johnny trying to cover up? Was it only Harold's
misdeeds—or was he also involved in something horrible?

Johnny had apologized to those poor children's families so they
could have closure, but the complete truth still has not been told.
Johnny was up to something. He was an evil man. I saw it in his eyes.
After what Harold did to all those poor people, I wondered what his
father had done to him. In my heart, I knew Johnny was a bad man.

I soon found out what an awful man Johnny was. I was watching
Johnny at Harold's house because I wanted to find out what he had

done. I also wanted to make sure he wasn't coming for me. I saw a mysterious person going in and out of Harold's house, but I couldn't tell who the person was. As I listened inside that haunted mansion house, I recognized my babysitter's voice. Anne and Johnny were fighting over money, and I eventually heard Anne being killed.

Johnny was arrested for the murder of Anne. I remember being happy when the police took him away in that police car.

I think about getting Gary and my beloved baby boys back. I am one blessed girl. I am in my happy place beside Gary. I will never forget what I have gone through, but it is nice to know everything turned out well for my family and me.

I am truly safe now, but I will never forget what I got myself into. Why am I so curious about things? Why do I always get myself into such bad situations?

CHAPTER TWO
WAKING UP WITH JOY

My dreams are not always so good. I still have the horrendous ones where I'm being chased—and someone is trying to get me. I still wake up screaming sometimes but not as much. Having bad dreams just reinforces that I need to keep up the therapy and medications. I also need to keep my faith close and never forget that God is always there for me. He will never leave me. I am slowly getting my joy back.

I roll over and hug Gary. He sleepily wakes and says, "Good morning, my love. You slept well last night, didn't you?"

I reply, "I had a dream last night, but it was a good one. Oh, Gary, I believe I've gotten my joy back. Let's get up and drink coffee together before you have to go to work."

He replies, "Sounds good to me. You know, you're the girl for me, right?"

"Gary, I've been thinking about everything that happened to me in the past few years. I hope nothing ever happens again to me like that," I say.

Gary says, "Rachael, just stick close to me, and I'll never let anything happen to you again. I'm so glad you are getting some relief from the bad dreams. Just keep going to therapy and taking your medicine. I believe it is helping, don't you?"

I reply, "I believe it is working. I try not to think about that time, but sometimes I can't get it out of my mind. I know that's bad for me. When I think about something, I normally dream about it."

Gary says, "Rachael, just keep your faith, and all will be good for us. Don't ever forget that you're my girl."

Gary gets up to get dressed for work. Every day, he looks so handsome. I'm so attracted to him. I can hardly keep my hands off him. He is the same way with me. We touch each other often, barely able to stop showing so much affection to each other.

I make him a breakfast sandwich to take with him. My breakfast sandwiches are so good. I put eggs, bacon, cheese, tomatoes, and lettuce on them. He always eats in the cafeteria at school at noon. He kisses me as he walks out the door. I hear the door open again; it's my Gary coming back inside for more kisses from me. I'm so blessed that he loves me so.

During the day, I watch the boys and do the house chores. I do the laundry and then clean the kitchen. After that, I vacuum the floors because I want the floor to be clean for James and John. I also make sure I never miss my therapy classes. I believe the therapy is helping me. It feels so good to see Mama and Dad often. They just adore getting to see our boys. I see Joe, my brother, when he visits them. I don't get to see Theresa and Veronica that much since they are still in college. I feel like my life is getting back to normal. I am living a good dream now, and I am very happy. Can it last?

After my ordeal with the murders and the commune, Gary and I went back to living together as man and wife. Our loving is so good, and we can hardly wait to get to see each other again. Gary is a good person and a Christian man. He prays with me at night and reads to Bible to me. Before he leaves the house in the mornings, he prays with me at the front door. Plus, he gives me all the kisses. He took me back after all we went through. I know he loves me with all his heart—just like I love him.

CHAPTER THREE

THE CALM BEFORE THE STORM

The biggest excitement after my ordeal was when I got to see my babies for the first time. I remember that day as I cautiously enter our old house. Everything is the same, and not one piece of furniture has been moved. Even the pictures of us and our babies are still there. Mama and Dad's pictures are in the same place where I hung them in the hallway. I am really shocked that Anne, our old babysitter, hasn't changed everything in my house.

As I enter the baby's room, I am so scared. Will they like me or even remember me? Will they scream because I am a stranger? I am their mother, but I left them for quite a while. That is all that matters to me. I need to get to know them again, and they need to get to know me.

As I walk into their room, they are playing with their toys on the floor. I bend down and get on the floor with them. They are laughing and having so much fun. I start playing with them. John throws a block at James, but no one gets hurt. I keep watching them. Every once in a while, they glance over at me, but they mostly stay focused on their toys. I don't think they recognize me as their mother, but they know I am nice. I don't try to hug them or force them into my lap. I keep smiling at them to let them know I am safe to be around.

Gary enters the room, and both boys jump up, run to him, and start hugging his legs. Gary starts laughing, pulls them into his arms, and hugs them. As he sits them down on the floor with the toys, James throws a toy at John. I laugh because they are acting like boys. They are always throwing things.

They start jabbering and repeating some words. They are so cute—like doll babies. I love them so much. I am amazed by how they have grown, but know I was gone for a while. I have guilt in my heart for missing part of their lives. I didn't even get to see them take their first steps. Was I a bad mother?

Gary says, "John, James, this is your mother. She is a nice Mama. She loves you."

John replies, "Mama."

James says, "No, Mama." He picks up a toy and throws it at me.

Gary tells him to be nice.

It is so cute. Tears are running down my face. What little miracles they are. I am so blessed to have them back in my life. I missed so much during those two years. They are walking and running everywhere and playing. I missed a good part of them growing up. They are tiny blessings to us.

Gary asks, "Do you want to get down and play with Mama?"

Both of them say, "No!" They stay in Gary's arms and say, "Da-Da."

It is precious to see how much he loves them and how attached they are to him. I feel like an awful mother because I left them. Bad things happen when you stick your nose where it shouldn't be.

No is their favorite word. Mama and Dad tell me they say no the best. This is part of being in the terrible twos. All they want to do is play with their toys all the time. They are such busy bees, and I am glad they have each other to play with. There is no greater miracle in my life than those two.

I laugh and say, "Gary, it's OK. Don't force them. They will come to me when they get comfortable."

He says, "Well, I'm putting them down to play with their toys. They are very heavy, especially holding both of them at the same time."

He tells them to play nice and not throw toys at each other. He tells them to not throw anything at me either. I just laugh.

I stay on the floor and play with my boys. They eventually play with me too. I knew they would get used to me. When one of them looks at me and says, "Mama," the other one also says it. They are both chubby and waddle as they walk. Mama bought them so many clothes. We will have to buy them bigger outfits soon since they are growing like weeds. They are just living dolls, and I am so proud to be back in their lives. I still worry that they will remember that I left them. I worry that they will be scarred by this.

Gary and I are so much in love and enjoy being with each other all the time. I don't want to go anywhere without him. We are finally settling down and getting back into our routine. The boys are very happy and are such a delight to be around. At night, they sleep well and rarely wake up. We are back on our honeymoon after being apart for two years. Gary goes to work, I watch the babies during the day, and our evenings are full of eating together and playing with them. Our nights are full of making love. Gary continues telling me every day that I'm his girl. I love hearing him say this.

My dreams are getting less scary and are not as bad. I hope I can control them. Therapy is going well, and I believe it is helping me work through some things in my life that I've always been worried about. I've always worried that someone was going to get me in the dark. I don't know where this comes from, but it's been this way since I was a little girl. I am learning to walk in the dark without being afraid of someone reaching out and getting me. I am learning about walking in the dark because I don't want to wake our boys during the night.

As we drift off to sleep in each other's arms, I start dreaming.

I'm being chased by a person with blood running down their arms and legs. I see a knife in their hand. I'm running toward the river and notice a large spider going toward the river. I am so frightened and have goose bumps running up and down my arms. I finally see his face, and it is the most frightful-looking person I've ever seen. I keep running from him.

Once I get to the river, I stop and see all my friends swimming as if nothing is happening. Sarah and Ryan are yelling at me to get in the water with them. I wake up as the spider touches my hand.

I awake frightened, but I go back to sleep immediately. My next dream is familiar.

Mama and I went to the grocery store in town. When we got home, we were putting away the groceries. Our front door suddenly opened. I looked up and stared right into the ugliest face I'd ever seen. He wore a big cowboy hat and a dusty black coat that flowed to his ankles. He was a tall man, taller than Dad, with a very large nose and a deep red scar over one dead eye. I whimpered as the cowboy grinned, reached under his coat, and pulled out a knife. My head whipped from right to left, but Mama was nowhere to be seen. The cowboy took a step and then paused to cough up a thick wad of blood. For a moment, he stared at it, and then he began to chuckle. My heart hammered so loud that I felt it in my ears. I wanted to run, but my breathing became shallow. I could hardly stand.

As I snatched a box of Lucky Charms from the kitchen table and fell to the ground.

The cowboy put one dirty boot on my chest. He paused and tapped the knife against his cheek, like he was thinking hard. I glanced back up and screamed in horror as the knife plunged down. I held the cereal box up like a shield. The knife slammed right into the smiling picture of Lucky, but the box held it back.

When the cowboy yanked the knife free, blood began to ooze from the box. The river that flowed down to the floor contained the usual marshmallows, green clovers, blue diamonds, yellow horseshoes—all of the Lucky Charms. However, they weren't green or blue or yellow; they were red, like tiny little organs. Vomit rushed to my mouth, and it erupted forth in a scream.

I'm screaming my head off, and Gary is trying to calm me down. He is holding me tightly.

"Rachael, wake up. It's just a dream. You're OK."

I'm crying. In my dream, I'm not sure if I was scared more of the bloody person or the spider. Why are my horrible dreams always about someone trying to get me? Why do they always include spiders, rats, and wolves that are trying to scare the daylights out of me. Is it because I'm so scared of them?

I'm so frightened as I tell Gary about my dream. I tell him that I actually had two dreams. The first one, of course, had my normal scary things in it, especially the large spider. I tell him how I drifted back to sleep and dreamed about the scary cowboy—a dream I had when I was a teenager.

He is trying his best to comfort me, but he is shaking all over too. He is holding me so tightly. I have scared him so much. When I do this to him, he always thinks someone has gotten me in our house or someone has broken in to steal our things.

I hear the boys crying. What a disaster going on in the middle of the night! I caused it with my terrible dreams. Will they ever end?

I say, "Gary, I'm so sorry I scared you and the babies. I'm going to get the boys back to sleep. Please try to go back to sleep. I'm so sorry." I jump out of bed as our babies are getting louder and louder. They are so frightened. I hate when I do this.

Gary replies sleepily, "It's OK. I'm going back to sleep. I'm kind of getting used to this, but I hope it doesn't continue every night. OK, Rachael?"

As I run out of our bedroom, I say, "OK, Gary. I'll try."

I eventually get the boys back to sleep. I rock both of them in my lap. It's a full load, but I love it. As I fall asleep, my dreams continue. This time, I dream about my babies.

I heard my babies crying. They were crying so hard. They were screaming their heads off in their cribs. They looked like small ghosts. They were white all over. I didn't make them a bottle to eat. I didn't want to. I was looking at them as if they were just baby dolls. They stayed in their beds all day and all night with no diapers or food. They were good babies. John and James were in the bathtub, and I took my eyes off them for one minute. They were facedown in the water. There was blood everywhere. Their floating toys were so bloody. A small fish jumped up out of the water, and I screamed. John and James were splashing and having fun again. They were OK.

I wake up so frightened and trying to understand my dream about my babies. My mind is so full of turmoil. I don't tell Gary because I don't want him to worry about my sanity. He will think I'm crazy and believe I might hurt them. I know in my heart that I will never hurt them. Would I neglect them? That would be bad also, right?

CHAPTER FOUR

LIFE AT THE RIVER GOES ON

Our friends still go to the river all the time for picnics, swims, and just plain fun. It is just like growing up a long time ago—without the murders, of course. In spite of our childhood friends being murdered, everything seems like it's back to normal. Most of our friends have at least one or two children. Kiddos are running around everywhere.

It is just like it used to be when Mama and Dad and all our neighbors got together, but they were older. We are now the adults, and we wait on our parents. It is their time to enjoy fun times and not have to do all the work.

Living back on the Nueces River, near Carrizo Springs, Texas, is so good. I love our small West Texas town, and our small community of families enjoys doing fun things all the time. We have events every weekend. This weekend, we have a fish fry, and all the guys cook for us. We have fried fish, hush puppies, fries, and onion rings. The ladies fix iced tea and fruit punch for everyone. It is so refreshing in the heat. Most of us float in the river to stay cool. Our children are splashing in the water. They are on a float or have floaties on their arms to keep them safe.

Mama asks, "Rachael, will you be able to go to the artesian well this week and get us some good water? Dad and I are almost out."

I laugh. "Sure, Mama. I know sinners like you and Dad need holy water!"

Dad says, "Rachael, don't be pointing fingers at us. You have three pointing right back at you."

Mama replies, "I know it is good enough to cook my fresh vegetables in. It makes them so tasty. We enjoy drinking it because we know it comes from a fresh spring. It is so clean and fresh. I love it."

I say, "I know, Mama. I will go next week. Don't forget that I'll be bringing the boys to you and Dad tomorrow. I have my therapy session."

She replies, "We'll be ready for them. It is so much fun playing with them. Taking care of grandkids is different. We can give them cookies and candy and then send them home. Maybe give them some red Kool-Aid, just kidding!"

Our weekends are so much fun. Everyone is off work and has fun together. Our friends are very nice, and we love doing things with them. We go to the river and have game nights. We sit around and play and laugh and have fun. It's sad when everyone has to go back to work.

Joe and Carol come to the river each weekend. They announce that they are having a baby, and everyone congratulates them. The whole town is happy for them. The ladies are already discussing how to give them a great baby shower.

Joe says, "I hope it is a girl—and she looks just like Carol."

Carol replies, "That's funny, Joe."

He replies, "Well, if it's a boy, and it looks like me, we are in big trouble. I'm not too pretty to look at."

Everyone laughs, and we all get up and hug them. It is so exciting to have more babies around. Mama and Dad are ecstatic about another grandchild. Our group is getting larger and larger. Everyone is so happy for them. I hope that watching three grandkids will not be too much for them. I know they are getting older.

As we are going home, I tell Gary that it will be nice to have another baby in the family.

He says, "I agree. One day, we should try for a girl. Who knows? We could have twin girls. What would we name them?"

I laugh as I ignore what he has just said. I think I've just gotten my boys back. "I'm attending my therapy session tomorrow in town."

He replies, "I hope it's helping you, Rachael, especially with the dreams."

The next day, I dropped the boys at Mama and Dad's house. My parents were glad to see them. They picked them up and took them to their playroom. Mama had turned a bedroom into a baby room with two cribs and toys everywhere.

I sit in the therapist's waiting room; I think about the bad dreams I've had my whole life. What made me be like this? Mama said I was scared of everything and hid behind her skirt when I was a little girl. I remember seeing things in my bedroom and staring at them. I once thought Jesus was standing at our bedroom door. The person never moved as I stared at it. I must have drifted off to sleep because when I awoke again, it was gone. I then laugh; it could have been my dad in his white underwear. Why do I have to be this way and be scared of everything?

I'm called to the back office to talk to my therapist. I avoid saying certain things to him. I don't want him to think I'm a crazy person. I tell him about my dreams, but I don't tell him they are just like horror movies. I play down everything to try to seem halfway normal.

Today, I decide to talk about my dreams from the past few nights. If I hold back too much, he will be able to see that I'm not opening up. I don't want him to know that I'm keeping secrets.

I say, "Spencer, this is why my bad dreams happen. Whatever I think about or hear someone say, I dream about it that night or in the next few days. Gary agrees with me. We don't watch scary movies at night. We don't watch them during the day either." I laugh. "Someone is always chasing me and trying to get me. I'm a grown woman, but I'm always scared a monster is going to get me."

He says, "It sounds like the power of suggestion really works with you. I'll be sure not to say anything about scary things in the dark. Just kidding. What else do you dream about?"

I reply, "Just about anything: spiders, snakes, rats, wolves. You name it—I dream that it's going to get me. Something is always chasing me—even clowns."

He replies, "Really? Tell me more about your dream last night."

I say, "I was on a hayride with all my friends, being pulled by a tractor. All around us, it was very dark. Out of nowhere, these giants started chasing us. They were tall and skinny. Their arms were going everywhere, up and down and then from side to side. I noticed that they were wearing stilts that made them so tall. They were coming very close to us. I threw myself into the middle of the trailer and hid under the hay. I was shaking all over as the spiders seemed to be everywhere. The tractor driver just laughed and took off very fast. It was just giants running after me, and a spider was trying to get me. When the spider touched my arm, I screamed and woke up Gary."

Spencer says, "I'm very sorry that you dream this way. Maybe, as we discuss more and more, you will feel released from this burden. I'm very educated in psychological dreaming issues, and talking about hurts, habits, and hang-ups has helped others. It should help you too."

As I leave my session, I remember that I must never tell him that I think I may have killed two people at the commune. I do not want to go to jail. I have children to raise and a good husband to take care of. I know it's not good to hold things back, especially things like that. Murder is not something you can ignore. I need to address this issue at some point in my life, but I need to keep this little secret to myself right now.

I remember that I need to work hard tonight to not dream. I don't want to scare Gary with another one of my nightmares. Maybe I can remain awake as long as I can. This is getting ridiculous. My screams scare him so badly. It's something that you don't get used to. Maybe I need to double up on my medication at night. My poor family has to put up with my outbursts at night. Why am I the way I am? I guess I'm not a good person. Maybe I need to pray more. Maybe I will calm down and not scare the whole freaking world.

CHAPTER FIVE
COMMUNE DREAMS

All was good, until it wasn't.

My bad dreams have started again—even though I'm staying awake at night and taking more medication. Dreaming scary things is the least of my worries now. You see, my dreams have evolved to my time at the commune and what happened to me there. I think about this time in my life day and night. I can't get it out of my mind. As Gary and I are getting ready for bed, I tell myself that I need to quit thinking about the things that happened to me then. They just make me dream more.

Gary says, "Rachael, please think about good things tonight. Think about our good boys and how they are healthy and doing so well. Don't think about what is in your past. The past is past, and I hope you can get over this."

I say, "Oh, Gary, I know I've got to think good thoughts and not dwell on the bad. I'm going to go to sleep tonight and not have any dreams at all. Can you pray with me and ask God to give me happy thoughts tonight?"

Gary says, "Dear God, help Rachael have good dreams tonight. Thank you in advance for your answered prayers."

I say, "Amen."

Gary says, "Rachael, try hard to sleep well. I have to work, and these sleepless nights are making me very tired. How did your parents and sisters and brothers take being awakened so much at night? I guess they had to. I can hardly get out of bed in the mornings."

"I'm so sorry, and I will try very hard. Maybe I need to sleep on the couch on some nights to give you some relief. I think I will start taking even more medication at night, and this might help."

With a stern look, Gary says, "I don't want you on the couch. I want you with me."

I smile as he says that. He's the guy for me.

However, as we get in bed, I have an uneasy feeling as I drift off to sleep.

I'm back at the commune again. I'm running through a building with blood on the walls. Blood is seeping underneath the baseboards. The bad abortion door is locked. As I run to it with my screwdriver, someone is right behind me. I look behind me, and even though I can feel their breath on my neck, no one is there. Maybe it is a ghost. It is so cold. As I look again, I see the door opening slowly. Cindy is on the stone-cold table. I touch her hand and feel how cold it is. I see Leader Charles with a clothes hanger in his hand. Jerry is standing beside him and smiling.

I see a man in the room. He is dressed all in white. I keep staring at him. Who is this? In my mind, I think it is Jesus since he is all in white. I really hope it is not Harold. I just lay there watching as hard as I can, trying to determine who it is. I can't move. If I do, they will know I am awake—and they will grab me. I recognize the man and see that he is a clown. The clown has a knife in his hand. He stops and turns his head around completely and continues to stare at me. He begins to laugh as am shaking. He says, "You're a scary-cat, aren't you?" I can't say anything. He says, "Did you see me kill?" I still can't say anything. I then see it is Harold, and he starts laughing at me. I turn around to run, and the clown slashes my arm. I look down and see blood and scream.

I wake up screaming, and Gary holds me and tries to calm me down. The whole bed is shaking. I can't stop. Gary doesn't know what to do with me. It's so good to be held by him. I drift back to sleep and wake up in the morning and remember the odd, scary dreams from the night before. There's no telling what I might dream. Things are all mixed up together.

I then hear James and John playing. I run into their room and play with them for a while. Gary has already left for work. I guess he wanted me to get some sleep. I eventually make breakfast for myself and the kids.

I try to forget my dream from the previous night, but it keeps bugging me all day. Why am I dreaming about the commune again? My life at the commune was horrible. I had to endure all the rapes and beatings, but it wasn't bad all the time. I enjoyed the worship time with them. I remember raising my hands to the Lord. I remember a preacher saying, "As you are lifting your hands toward heaven, Jesus is touching your hands." The worshipping was good, but the other stuff there was bad.

Is there significance to this dream? Will I go back there someday?

CHAPTER SIX

THERAPIST WOES

I continue attending my classes twice a week with my therapist, Spencer. It's not so bad. I have been discussing my night terrors and what happened to me at the commune for many months now. As I said before, I can't tell him everything. He has many framed licenses and certificates on his wall. I know he is not a doctor, but it looks like he sure is smart. He is helping me walk through my terrible ordeals. We talk about my dreams, or nightmares, as I like to call them. We talk about being at that horrible commune. I notice that he looks like a nerd with his wire-rimmed glasses hanging from his nose. I guess he's in the right field of work. He sure looks like a Poindexter type of guy. I think, *Don't all psychiatry professionals look like this?*

He seems truly interested in working with me, and he is very knowledgeable about my issues. He talks about my dreams and why they could possibly be happening to me. He knows I'm taking medication that helps me sleep, be happy, and have fewer dreams. I'm just getting to where I trust him, and I am opening up and telling him more. However, I still haven't told him that I possibly killed two people, Cindy and Jerry, at the commune. I lived there for two years. I have to keep this secret. If I told him, wouldn't he turn me in to the authorities and have me arrested for murder? I don't want to go to jail. I just can't leave my family again; my heart couldn't take it. My two little boys are just beginning to trust me and love me as their mother.

"Good morning, Rachael. I hope all is well today," Spencer says.

I sit down in one of his comfy chairs and immediately start talking. I guess this is what they want their patients to do.

"I had a bad dream about the commune last night. I was back there again, and it was so vivid, actually bloody. Just thinking about it right now gives me chills up and down my arms. I woke myself up screaming, and of course. Gary. That poor man of mine. I was so scared that my body was shaking all over. You see, in my dream, I was back in the House of Blood, and they had Cindy tied down on a table. It was so real. I saw blood all over the walls, rolling down them like a river. Leader Charles and Jerry were there too. They looked so angry, and they were smirking. They are both so wicked. What do you think this dream means, Spencer? Am I going back there? Please tell me I won't go back there ever again."

Spencer says calmly, "Rachael, I can't tell you that you will never return. I can't predict these kinds of things. I certainly hope you never go back there, for sure."

I reply, "There's only one thing that could take me back there. I still have the small car that belonged to Cindy, and I need to return it to her. I don't want to be charged for theft."

"I know you are scared, but you need to return that car as soon as possible. Why aren't you getting the police involved? At least get Gary to help you. They both will surely understand what needs to be done."

"You are right. I will talk to Gary about that tonight. Maybe I can get Gary to return it for me. Oh, gosh! Someone will have to follow me there when I drop it off—so I will have a ride home. This will be risky to avoid those people seeing us."

I continue talking to Spencer about the commune and how scared I still am of that place.

"Rachael, I know you are scared, but you need to face your fears."

Haven't I already faced enough fears for a lifetime? However, I knew I had to face my fears when I was thrown into the House of Blood. It was a horrible time for me. Does Spencer know about the commune and all the houses? I'm starting to be leery of him. He seems to know too much about it. Am I being paranoid—or does he know more than he is saying? I think I should watch what I say again and not tell him everything.

Spencer says, "Rachael, tell me more about what happened to you in the House of Blood. You are always telling me about the building. What happened there? Did you see something in there that scares you? Are you worried that someone will come after you? Tell me what happened to you in that building. Did they do horrible things to you in there?"

I reply, "I can't talk about some of the things that happened to me at the commune. It is just too soon." My mind wonders as I remember the torture.

Spencer then says, "Rachael, you must tell me if you injured or killed someone there. We have talked enough about the commune for now, but you need to try to remember things. I think your mind has blocked the memories. I know bad things happened there to you. I just need to know."

I say warily, "I'm innocent. I can't talk about anything I did there."

He says, "Is it because you could be arrested if anyone found out what you did?"

I scream at him, "Please leave me alone—and do not go down that road of trying to accuse me of anything illegal. You are out of line. Are you trying to get me in trouble?"

Spencer replies calmly, "No. As your therapist, I need to get everything out in the open so that you can heal your mind, body, and soul. Always remember that you are covered under patient confidentiality."

"No, you're just trying to get me arrested," I say nervously.

He then says, "Are you saying that you did something there that would send you to jail? Are illegal activities going on there?"

Suddenly, it comes to me. He knows more about the commune than he is letting on. He is trying to trick me. Was he ever there? Does he work for them? Maybe he sends people there when they need help facing their fears. I am very suspicious of him now. He seems to know too much. He can't stop talking about what goes on at the commune. In my prior sessions with him, he talked about the buildings. I didn't tell him very much about them. How does he know so much about them? Does he know Leader Charles?

I then repeat myself to Spencer, saying, "I did not do anything."

Spencer then changes the subject and asks about being home and fitting in with my family. He knows he has gone too far with me.

I am so glad that we are done talking about the commune. I do not trust him, and I need to be careful that he doesn't trick me into saying things I shouldn't. He seems to know about communes. Does he know about my commune? I know he changed the subject because he was telling me too much about it. Is he working for them?

Spencer then asks, "Rachael, tell me about your last dream. Does anyone ever catch you? As you have described your dreams to me, whoever is chasing you never really catches you. You always wake up before that happens, right?"

I reply, "Yes, that is true. I wake up before someone catches me. However, the other night, the spider touched my hand. I was sure it was a brown recluse, and it was going to bite me, but it didn't. I had heard when they bite, the human skin rots. I didn't like spiders at all. Why do I always wake up when something bad is about to happen?"

Spencer replies, "Yes, human nature doesn't let the bad things or bad people harm us in our subconscious. It is a built-in safety mechanism that keeps us sane."

I say, "Well, I'm glad for that. I'm glad the spider didn't bite me."

Spencer glances at his watch and says, "Rachael, your time is up for today. I think we had a good talk. Please keep coming and talking through your fears. I believe it will really help you. Don't forget to make your follow-up appointment. I'll see you again next week."

"Thank you, Spencer. I believe it is helping also," I reply.

I leave my therapist's office and am very confused and conflicted about Spencer. Is he a good guy—or is he trying to get me arrested? For all I know, he could be working for Leader Charles and will take me back there any day now. I'm so suspicious of that little Poindexter guy.

In my next session, I'm going to try to find out if Spencer has ever been to a commune, including the commune I was at. Maybe some of his other patients have been to the commune. He probably won't tell me jack. I don't know, but I'm very leery of Spencer.

CHAPTER SEVEN
COMMUNE INVESTIGATIONS

After therapy, I pick up John and James from Mama and Dad and hurry home to cook dinner for Gary. I want to cook him something good to make up for keeping him awake during my horrible dreams the night before. While I cook his favorite meal, I think about today's session with my therapist. Is it really helping me?

Gary arrives home, kisses me, and says, "Hi, honey. Did you have a good session today?"

I say, "Yes, it was good. We talked about how when I'm dreaming, I'm facing my fears. I've cooked you chicken-fried steak, mashed potatoes, green beans, and hot rolls. Mama made extra homemade yeast rolls just for you. I know it's your favorite meal!"

"Thanks, Rachael. What are you trying to do, get me in the sack, honey? Don't worry … it's a done deal. I hope the sessions are helping you work through your issues with your dreams. I'm so tired, honey. You have to work hard during these sessions so that you can stop having these night terrors—or at least slow them down. I'm tired."

"I'm so sorry for waking you up. I wish I didn't suffer from these horrible dreams. It makes my nights so hard also. I know you don't really understand why I am the way I am. I've endured these night-mares for as long as I can remember … my poor family and now you. I've always been so scared of everything. I wouldn't even let my dad pick me up and hold me in his arms. I would just scream. I only wanted my Mama. I promise, Gary, I will try harder."

After I get the boys to sleep, I go to our bedroom. Gary wants to talk about my time at the commune a lot. He thinks I'm still suf-fering from my ordeal. I want to not think about those things right now. I make love to Gary tonight to relax him and get his mind off my dreams. If I show my love for him, he will see that I am trying to get better. We make love, and I feel at peace as I drift off to sleep.

Cindy and Jerry are chasing me down a long road that leads to the dark river. I slip and fall to the ground. As I get up, they start laugh-ing at me and telling me I'm a klutz. I look at their clothes and see dried blood on them; it is even on their shoes. What have they done? Is this blood where I stabbed them? I'm so scared, and I start running again. They chase me into the river, and rats are everywhere in the water. They begin laughing at me again as the rats begin biting my arms and legs. These rats' eyes are lit up and glowing in the dark. Cindy and Jerry are still on the bank watching. I notice there is no blood on their clothes now. I can't figure out where the blood went. As Cindy and Jerry enter the water, they reach out and grab me. I'm fighting them, and my arms are thrashing in the water. My head is going in and out of the black, murky water. I think I'm going to drown as I scream loudly. In my dream, I see myself near death. I just close my eyes in terror.

I wake up, but I do not scream. I'm not sure why I don't scream. Maybe it's because I was screaming in my dream so much. Thank the Lord for this. I'm so glad I didn't wake up my Gary. I can hear his slow breathing in his sleep.

I am so confused by this dream, and as I lay there, I start thinking about it. Did I kill Cindy and Jerry? Are they still alive and well? I need to investigate this and get it settled once and for all. After I left the commune, I had a bag with a bloody knife and dress in it. What happened to it? Did I do something with it? Did my dad find the evidence and remove it from my car so I would not get in trouble? I hoped it was a dream. I hope Jerry and Cindy are OK.

I start to pray and find my comfort with the Lord.

CHAPTER EIGHT
THE SNEAKINESS CONTINUES

Without telling Gary, at least once per week, I started leaving James and John with Mama and Dad for an extended period of time. They were already keeping them for short visits when I went to therapy. I tell them I was having extended therapist sessions that involved my dreaming issues. I told them it was like having a sleep study, but I would be gone for most of the day. I was still meeting with my therapist, Spencer, once a week. I knew Mama and Dad believed me. What a liar I am.

What I was really doing was driving two hours to the commune to see if Cindy and Jerry were alive. I needed to find out if I was a murderer. I could potentially be arrested at some point in my life if I didn't find out for sure.

As I think about that last day at the commune, I can't remember any of the details other than seeing them in the bed together and getting so mad. I was so jealous that I could have killed them. Did I do it or not? This is driving me crazy, and I need to find out.

Cindy's car needs to be driven anyway, and it is so small that I think I can hide it better. I remember all the willow trees they had around the commune. This small car will be a piece of cake to hide. However, I guess I'm worried about hiding the car. I can't drive Cindy's yellow car too close to the commune because they will recognize it. Anyone would be suspicious if they saw a car parked for a long time, especially Cindy's car. It would raise so many red flags.

As I continue driving toward the commune, I think about what I am going to investigate today. I must be careful since the commune already has troubles with TV reporters investigating them, and they will be on the lookout for nosy people like me. I remember the reporters while I was staying there.

I look down at my feet and see my sneakers. Here I go again, sneaky Rachael. I can get myself into some fixes, but I don't care. I've got to figure out if I'm a murderer or not. I pull up to a park that is about a mile from the commune. The park is very old and has many weeds. Since the car is so small, I park behind a large willow tree. Since I can't see the car, I know the commune people won't be able to see it either. I second-guess myself and think, *Is this too close? Will they find me?* I confidently tell myself that I'm not too close. I will be very careful—just like when I was investigating at the river and at Harold's old house. I will be very discreet and quiet, and no one will see me. I have to keep telling myself this so I feel safe.

I walk slowly through the eerie woods and approach back of the commune. Maybe no one will see me watching them. It's a good spot. I sit behind a large willow tree and take out my binoculars. My brother used to think he was an investigator. He even asked Dad if he could have a gun. Joe is currently an investigator for the police department in our town. He would kill me if he knew what I am doing. At least he gets a gun now. I laugh to myself.

With my binoculars, I look around as much as I can. I need to find a better location where I can see more. All I can see is the back of the canteen where all the followers go to eat. As I'm sitting quietly in my hiding place, Cook comes out the back door and throws out some water. I cautiously sit behind my tree, not moving, so she cannot see me. If I get caught, there's no telling what they will do to me.

I sit there for about an hour, and when my legs start to fall asleep, I go back to the small yellow car. As I'm driving home, I think I will definitely go back next week for some more investigating. I still need to find out if Jerry and Cindy are alive. I want to return Cindy's car and not get in trouble for stealing it. You can go to jail for theft and murder. These two things, if they are true, will put me in jail. I need to carefully return my stolen car as soon as possible. I desperately need to find out if I killed Jerry and Cindy.

I have this yearning inside. I want to make Leader Charles suffer for what he did to me. If Jerry is still alive, he also needs to be punished for what he did. I need to get rid of two very evil people. Both of these men hurt me very badly, and they need to pay.

What is wrong with me? Aren't I a Christian? Do I have evil living in me? Why do I have these thoughts? I start praying to the Lord, asking for forgiveness for my bad thoughts. If I had enough sense, I would stay out of this and let the police take care of matters. But, no, that's not my style. I know I've got to put my nose into things that end up getting me into trouble. Why do I have to be this way? So many flaws. It reminds me of the song "Flawless," which says, "No matter the hurt, or how deep the wound is, no matter the pain, still the truth is, the cross has made you flawless." I must never forget this.

CHAPTER NINE
CHURCH ENCOURAGEMENT

I pick up the boys from Mama and Dad and head to the house. I need to quit thinking such evil thoughts. I especially need God's help to not get caught while I'm investigating. I need to get closer to God and have his assurance in my heart. I need to restore my body and soul at church. There are so many needs in my life right now. Going to church always brings me comfort and encouragement.

Luckily, it is a Wednesday, and we have church tonight. I need to be filled with God's promises and his Word. Oh, God, please restore my soul and save me from the dangerous situations I get myself into.

When Gary comes home from work, I have sandwiches and chips ready for him. I've already fed the boys ravioli, which they love. We don't have much time before church starts so I hadn't prepared a large meal. I can't wait to be around other Christians at our church. Everyone is so nice and friendly. I just know that church will keep me from the evil thoughts that invade my mind. I can't wait to hear what our pastor will preach tonight. I need praise and worship in my life right now. I just know it will help me with my dreaming. It did before, and the Lord can do it again.

Gary says, "Rachael, you seem very excited about church tonight. What's going on? Are they having something special tonight?"

I say, "No, I need to be closer to God and walk in His way. I believe this will help me with my bad dreams. I can't wait to see all our friends and catch up on what's going on. You know we never gossip, right?"

Gary laughs and says, "I hope the good Lord does help you, Rachael. I'm not mad at you for dreaming, but I wish your night terrors would stop."

"I agree with you, Gary. I'm so sorry for keeping you awake."

As we enter the church, I can feel the presence of the Lord. I am struggling with the bad dreams more frequently. I am also dealing with some scary and exciting times as I investigate. We all have different seasons in life, some good and some bad. Right now, I have some not-so-great ones going for me. I can't share anything with Gary or my congregation friends because they would think I am crazy and put me in the nuthouse. This is a secret I must keep to myself. The less people know about my investigations, the better. I think again about the seasons in my life. Some people are put in our lives for a season, some for a reason, and some of them for a lifetime. I sure hope Gary has been put in my life for a lifetime. He is the love of my life.

Worshipping with songs is awesome. When it's time for the Word, our Pastor reads Psalm 16:8 from the King James Version Bible: "I have set the Lord always before me; because he is at my right hand, I shall not be moved." It is as though he is preaching right at me today. The verse tells me that the Lord is always near me and that nothing can shake me. Is this a sign that I should proceed with my endeavors and not feel bad about going back to the commune to find answers? Is God telling me I won't get caught?

I don't believe God wants me to do evil toward Leader Charles and Jerry to pay them back. Maybe I should ask Detective Dale and Joe to help me to bring them to justice. I don't want to go to jail. I don't want the law involved until I can prove what is going on at that horrible commune. I just need to check on Jerry and Cindy. Are they still alive?

As Gary and I get the boys in bed, I say, "I loved church tonight. I feel so close to the Lord now. It's like I got my battery recharged, and I'm ready for anything. Listening to sermons like that encourages me about my dreams."

Gary replies, "Well, he did say that the Lord is always before us. At night, just think good thoughts. Try seeking God's face when you pray. In Leviticus, it says that we are to seek his face and turn from our sin, and he will heal our land."

I reply, "That's very good advice from our pastor and also from you, Gary. I hate that I dream and wake my whole family. I've done it my whole life. All you have to do is ask Joe about my childhood, and he will just roll his eyes. Now, I don't know what Veronica will say about them since she slept with me my whole life. Knowing her, she probably will laugh and tell a good story about me."

CHAPTER TEN

THE NIGHT TERRORS CONTINUE

As we are getting ready for bed, I talk to Gary about working at our church. Evelyn, my friend, told me they are going to renovate the fellowship hall. I had helped Dad redo his garage, and I would like to get out of the house and help someone. I am only taking care of the boys and going to therapy. I'm thinking helping at the church would give me another reason to be out of the house—and another excuse to go to investigate the commune. My mind is so twisted.

Gary says, "Rachael, I don't care what you do. I think keeping busy will be good for your mind. Go for it, girl!"

"Thanks for being so understanding. You are the best husband in the whole world, and I love you so much!"

"Rachael, please be careful when you work. I don't want you to get hurt. Watch for nails. Don't step on them. They will cause a bad infection. You would have to have a tetanus shot, for sure. Maybe the physical labor will make you so tired that you won't dream at night. I know you can't help it, but it gets old when you wake me up all the time."

"Gary, I can start sleeping on the couch. I did it at the commune and avoided getting in trouble for waking up anyone. I don't mind doing it. I want you to get the rest you need."

"Rachael, I want you in our bed with me. I love holding you in my arms at night. Just keep going to therapy and taking your medication. You're getting better."

I know he isn't telling me the truth. I'm not getting better with all the possible situations that I create on my own.

As we drive into the yard, after church, I see the yellow car behind the carport. I need to return it soon. I don't want to get arrested for stealing a car. However, the most important thing is that I don't want to get caught by those horrible people at the commune. I think Leader Charles would kill me.

I bathe the boys and put on their little pajamas. I put them in their small trundle beds. They are so good and go right to sleep. I guess they are tired from playing with all the other children at the church day care.

Gary is already in bed and waiting for me. I know he is so tired, so there won't be any loving tonight. I get ready and crawl under the sheets. I still have the phobia that I have to be covered up or someone will grab me in the night. I know it's a crazy thing in my head, but it's still there as an adult. It's something I will live with for the rest of my life. Gary leans over sleepily, holds me for a minute, and then kisses me good night.

As I am drifting off to sleep, I hear something outside. I don't want to wake Gary. I don't move. I listen with all my heart to see if I hear it again. I know a Peeping Tom is lurking outside our window. My imagination is going wild, but then I hear it again. I'm frozen in bed, not daring to move. I hear Gary's snoring softly. I keep listening for the sounds outside. At some point, I fall asleep to the dreams in my head.

My brother, Joe, has been buried alive, and I'm responsible for it. Joe and I went down to the pasture at our old homeplace. We are digging between the big barn and the pig barn. Joe digs so deep that he finds a tunnel. He enters the tunnel and goes down into a big hole. I go back to the house and leave him there. Later that night, Dad asks me where Joe is. I tell him what we were doing and that Joe is still in the ground. Dad's face gets so angry, and he yells at me that we have to dig him out. He is probably being smothered to death. We run down to the pasture and start digging. As we dig, more sand and dirt fill up the hole. Dad keeps telling me that Joe is dead. We keep digging, and we can't find him. Terror fills my heart as I drift into another dream about my brother.

I'm at the river, and we are all swimming. Joe walks up to me with something in his hand. I look, and it is a dead mouse. It has blood all over it. Joe laughs at me and says it is not real. I then see a knife and start stabbing a rat, over and over, in my hand. Mama comes up to me and tells me to stop—or she will spank me. I look at the rat, and the knife has disappeared. I stare at the rat, and it runs away. Joe runs up to me and yells, "Boo!" I scream in my dream.

As I awake from these weird dreams, I wonder why they are about Joe. Did we ever find him in the tunnels? Is something bad going to happen to him? I hope not. Joe is making something of himself.

After I was rescued from the commune, Joe went to school to become a private investigator. He is still married to my friend Carol. I remember how jealous I was when they started dating. She was my friend, and he was taking her away from me. I sure hope nothing happens to Joe. I drift off to sleep again into another dream.

Mama and I go to the grocery store. When we get home, we put the groceries away in the kitchen. I look up and see a man—all dressed in black—open the front door and step inside. This scary man has cowboy boots and a hat, but he does not look like any cowboy I have ever seen. His face looks so evil and ugly. His eyes are dark, beady, and bloodshot. Is he even alive? He has dirt all over his clothes and looks like a ghost. Has he come back from the grave to kill us? Is he a lunatic? Why does he have a switchblade? If he is a cowboy, why doesn't he have a gun?

I am trying to figure out how to save us. I know he is going to kill us, and I am so afraid. I am shaking all over, and the hair on my arms rises. I am petrified. This is the most nerve-racking situation I have ever been in. Mama is staring at him.

I see a large box of cereal on the table. It's Post Toasties this time, my Dad's favorite cereal. If I throw it at him, it will kill him. He cannot murder us if I kill him first.

He is walking toward us slowly.

We are going to be murdered if I don't do something right now. I picked up the cereal box, but my arms turn to Jell-O. I drop the box. He is coming toward us, closer and closer, and I scream.

I wake up screaming. I had the same dream when I was a child, and now I keep having it. As a kiddo, I woke my whole family up because I was screaming so loudly. Go figure, but I was actually sleeping on a cot in our living room. My older sister, my brother, and I were going to church camp the next day. My little sister, Veronica, was staying at my aunt's house because she was too young to go to camp. After the horrendous dream, Mama ended up putting me in bed with Theresa, and I shook her whole bed. I was so cold, and I needed more covers on me. None of us got much sleep that night. I thought the bad cowboy was coming back to get me. I didn't sleep for the rest of the night. I couldn't wait for daylight.

Gary is holding me and rocking me back and forth. "It's OK, Rachael. You will be fine. It was just another bad dream."

"No, Gary. It was horrible. It was a dream I had when I was a child. Why did I dream it again? It was terrible."

"Our brains are funny, Rachael. We never forget things, and they can come back to us in our dreams."

"No, Gary. It was exactly the same. How could I remember it so clearly? It was the same way when I was a kid. That cowboy looked the same, and he was trying to kill Mama and me. I have goose bumps all over my body."

He whispers, "Hush, Rachael. You will be fine. Just put your head on my shoulder, let me hold you to get you warm. Try to go back to sleep. It will be OK."

"OK." I quietly drift back to sleep.

CHAPTER ELEVEN
THE END OF SPENCER

When I wake up, Gary has already gone to work. The boys are awake. I hear them crying and fussing about something. I run to their room, and they have gotten out of the daybeds and are fighting over a toy. There are toys everywhere. You would think they have plenty to go around between them.

I laughingly say, "Good morning, boys. Are you hungry?"

They look at me and say, "Pancakes!"

I laugh. "Yes, I will make you pancakes."

As I'm cooking the pancakes, I remember my dreams from the night before. I sure hope nothing happens to Joe. He is a good brother, and he loves the law and investigating criminals. I know he is glad that he can carry a gun now. He's always wanted to do that. My dream about the cowboy was horrible also. Why am I having the cowboy dream over and over?

I put the boys in their high chairs, and they eat their pancakes. I need to get them cleaned up as soon as possible since I have an appointment with my therapist. I hope he doesn't ask me any more questions about the commune. He has been bugging me about that. Maybe I'll tell him about my bad dreams. I bet he'll have a lot to say about my evil cowboy dream.

I drop off the boys at Mama and Dad's house. They are always so excited to see their grandparents. We have taught them to call them Grandmommy and Granddaddy. They start yelling in glee as soon as I open the door. Mama and Dad are waiting for them with open arms. They always have special toys for them, and Mama buys their favorite juice and cookies. Dad enjoys walking them outside and showing them his new garage. He is so proud of it. John and James always have a blast over there. They even fuss a little when they have to go home. I've seen them throw themselves down on the ground, throwing a fit, because they want to stay.

As I enter my therapist's office, Spencer is standing by his window. I wonder if he watched me get out of my car. I'm suspicious of him now, and I think he may be involved with the commune people. I'm going to try to trick him into telling me something about that. I have to be careful because he is a very smart man.

I sit in my normal chair, and he sits across from me. He asks how my dreams have been going and how many I have been having. I tell him about a few of them, and he raises his eyebrows. I wonder if he thinks I'm doing better. I hope he doesn't recommend that I be admitted anywhere. I don't want him making up something about me that gets me in trouble.

I spend a lot of time telling him about the evil cowboy. I ask him if it is normal to have the same dream again.

Spencer replies, "Yes, our minds are like big storage files. We file things in them, and we sometimes go back to the files and open them again. It's not abnormal, and you may do it again. Please don't worry about that."

I reply, "I guess so."

"Rachael, what do you dream about the commune? I know you want to talk about your bad dreams, but we need to find out about the commune. Do you remember where it is and how to get there?"

"I really don't remember where the commune is. I was frightened out of my mind trying to get away from a killer. I'd say, it took about two hours to get there. Cindy talked so much that I didn't pay much attention to where we were going. I remember about fifty followers lived there. Do you know anyone who has ever been there?"

Spencer replies, "Yes, I had another patient a long time ago … I believe it was the same place where you stayed."

"Spencer, do you know how to get to this commune? Are you not telling me what you know?"

"No, I don't know this commune where Leader Charles and Jerry are. However, I believe it is the same one that my other patient told me about, but I don't know for sure. I heard there were rituals going on out there. Think hard, Rachael. Do you know where it is? I think it's important that you return that car before you get into trouble. You said it was about two hours from here. Which direction was it?"

I know that Spencer knows more about this place than he is saying. He asks so many questions, which makes me suspicious. I think he is asking me where the commune is to see if I can get back there. He probably is talking to Leader Charles about me. He keeps asking where it is, but I think he already knows.

This therapist is turning out to be a pain, and I need to be very cautious about what I say around him. I can't wait to get away from his office.

As I am leaving, Spencer says, "Rachael, if you remember anything about the commune, please let me know. I believe it will help with your bad dreams, especially the ones about the commune. I will see you next week."

"I think I'm doing better, and I may not need therapy any longer. What do you say about me only coming every other week?"

He says, "Rachael, don't forget that you are traumatized and need my help in working through this. Don't stop coming to see me. You still need help working through your dreams. Don't give up on this process. It will take time."

"I don't think so. Things are getting so much better."

"I'll see you next week—make that appointment at my front desk. You still need help."

Why does Spencer ask me so much about the commune? Does he want me to go back there? I will return the car as soon as I can. Maybe he can't wait until I go to jail. I wonder if Spencer used to live there. He can't stop questioning me. I don't think he is a very good therapist. He needs to stay out of my business.

Walking out that door feels like freedom. I know I am not going to return. I will not tell Gary or my parents that I am not going back to therapy. I don't need it anymore. Spencer is trying to get too close to me, and he is asking questions that I am not comfortable answering. I need time to investigate the commune. I need to find some answers. Spencer needs to leave me alone. I no longer trust him. He is history now.

As I'm driving home, I think about how lucky I am to have a good husband like Gary. He is the love of my life. He doesn't beat me for having bad dreams like the commune people did. He truly loves me, and he holds me to calm me down. The next time I go to the doctor, I'm going to ask if I can start taking even more medicine at night to try to prevent the horrific dreams. Maybe they can give me something stronger. I don't want Gary to start getting mad at me. I couldn't take it if he screamed and beat me like they did at the commune. Those were such bad people there.

I think, *I hope I don't dream tonight.* It's a thought that has crossed my mind almost every night of my life.

CHAPTER TWELVE

BLOODY NIGHT TERRORS

Someone has attacked me, and blood is rolling down my eyes. An eagle is trying to cut my eyes out. I'm running fast, and I trip. I fall to the ground. I look up and see that Harold has Sarah and Ryan tied to a tree beside the river. Their eyes have been cut out. He has sewn buttons over their eyes, but blood is dripping from underneath them. I jump up and keep running. I trip again. As I get up, Harold comes closer to me with a knife. He reaches for me, and I grab a box of cereal to throw at him. As I scream, my arms turn to Jell-O. I then hear someone following me as I am coming home from the river. I remember each step that he took as the leaves are crunching behind me. I feel the cold knife in my hand, and I know I will kill whoever is behind me. It is him or me—and I feel no remorse or fear at this point. I turn around and face my killer. It is Harold, of course. I stab him in the throat.

I wake up screaming.

Gary grabs me, and holds me, and tries to calm me down.

I can't stop crying. "I've never dreamed about an eagle before. The bad eagle was trying to claw out my eyes. The dream was so real. I have dreamed about throwing a box of cereal at a bad guy to kill him. It was me and Mama in that dream. Instead of a scary cowboy trying to get us, it was Harold. He was following me home, and I stabbed him in the throat. My mind is so twisted, Gary. I don't know what to do."

Gary says, "Rachael, are you still taking your medicine?"

"Yes, I am. I promise. Gary, I don't miss taking it. I'm sorry I keep waking you up. I've been this way my whole life. Please don't stop loving me or start hitting me."

"Rachael, I won't. I'm not one of those mean people at that commune. Please just hush up, and let's try to go back to sleep."

I whisper, "Gary, I'm so sorry. I will call my doctor tomorrow to see if I can get stronger medicine. The night terrors keep coming, and they are getting worse."

"OK, my dear. That sounds like a plan. Let's go back to sleep." He grabs me and holds me against his chest. This is truly my happy place.

The alarm goes off, and I jump up to make Gary coffee and breakfast. I know he can take it with him. He always sleeps until the last minute. I want to take extra care with him so that he can forgive me for waking him so many times during the night. Last night's dream was so frightening.

"Rachael, it's Friday. I have a board meeting tonight at school. I will be home late."

"That's OK. Mama and Dad are keeping the boys today. I'm going to work at the church. I need church bad after my horrible dreams last night."

Gary laughs as he walks out the door. "Well, you're probably right about needing the Lord to help you. He is always there. He will never leave you or forsake you. Bye, Rachael. Have fun today!"

I know it is wrong, and I hate lying to Gary, but I need to take another trip to the commune. Of course, Mama and Dad will keep the boys for me. I will be going to church on Sunday, and I will be sure to pray and ask God to forgive me. I need answers to my ordeals at the commune. I need to find out if Jerry and Cindy are alive. I cannot find the bloody knife and dress I dreamed about, so maybe I didn't kill them. One day I will return that car.

I hope no one finds out about my trips to the commune. If my family finds out, they will be so disappointed in me. If Leader Charles and Jerry find out, they will kill me.

CHAPTER THIRTEEN
COMMUNE SCRUTINY

I drop the boys at Mama and Dad's house. I tell them that I'm having another sleep study and will be gone most of the day. If they knew the truth, they would be so upset with me. I hate lying to them, but this is something that I have to do. I cannot keep myself from investigating the commune. I have to find out the truth about that awful place. Mostly, I need to find out if I'm a murderer.

Mama and Dad don't mind and are just so proud to be keeping the boys.

Mama says, "Get going, Rachael. You don't want to be late for your study. We will be just fine with these little guys."

Daddy says, "Come on, munchkins. Let's go play."

They laugh and run after their granddaddy. They love coming over here. I know Mama and Dad are proud that I'm getting help with my horrendous dreams. They have known all about them since I was a little girl. How can I ever repay them for what they did for me during those long scary nights in my childhood?

Now, they are helping me with my boys. I can't get over how much they have done for me in my life. Family is everything. In the long run, that's who will always have your back and love you to the end.

I stop by my house and pick up Cindy's yellow car. It's small, and it can be hidden easily. I need this alone time to work out some things for myself. I drive to the park and hide the car behind the bush. I've got my sneakers on, and I retrace my steps though the woods.

I wish I could repay Leader Charles and Jerry for what they did to me. They beat me, raped me, and nearly killed me—and Jerry and Cindy slept together behind my back. They all need to pay for what they did.

Even though I go to church, I have evil in my heart against these people. They belong to Satan, and I will be doing something good if I expose them. They need to be punished for what they do at the commune. The authorities need to throw them in jail and throw away the key.

After I find out if I'm a murderer, I will have to get the authorities involved. I can't take them down myself. What if they haven't done enough to be prosecuted? They beat and raped me. They have marijuana at the commune. They do unlawful abortions there. I don't know if they buy and sell drugs or do other bad things. When I figure it all out, I'll go to the law.

I find a hiding place in a different part of the commune. I'm being as careful as I can be, but I'm still nervous. I hide near one of the commune houses. It is called the "House of Peace." It was a good house, and I lived in it for a while. It gave me peace while I was figuring out my life. I was away from my husband, my babies, and my family. I missed them so much. At least I got to stay in a good building for a while. If Leader Charles hadn't gotten mad at me for my bad dreams, I could have stayed there. I wouldn't have been beaten and raped. Even Jerry, the guy who said he loved me, beat me.

I kept watching with my binoculars. A couple comes out of the House of Peace, and it looks like Jerry and Cindy. I need to get closer to make sure it's them. I need to know if I'm a murderer. I don't know why it is so important for me to come back here, but being a murderer is a good enough reason. I don't want to be guilty of killing them. I have to find out. If this means I'm putting myself in harm's way, then so be it. I need to find out.

When I found Jerry and Cindy in the bed together, it seemed like a dream. I have to find out if I killed them. I hope I had murder in my heart and turned around and walked out the door. They were having sex in the House of Peace. They were thrashing at each other like wild animals. I vaguely remember taking a knife and slicing them to death. If I really did it to them, they both deserved it. I think it would be impossible since Jerry would have gotten up the minute he saw me. He would have raped and beaten me right then. I guess I was so upset that I ran outside to Cindy's car. I had to get away quickly.

I sneak closer and sit under a tree. I'm not making a sound, and I'm barely breathing. I'm so scared, but I keep watching. I see a few followers I'm familiar with and a few new people. It wasn't that bad a place until I got in trouble. It was a safe place that I had to go to. I had to get away from Harold after I witnessed him murdering my childhood friends. I had to come back to investigate. I'm brave when it comes to finding out the truth.

I fall asleep under my safe tree.

I'm running toward our beloved river and being chased by Harold. As I turn around to see how close he is, he grabs my arm. I scream and shake loose from him, and I keep running. Johnny and Anne are also chasing me. Anne is holding a bloody knife. She stabs Johnny in the stomach, but he doesn't seem to be hurt. He keeps chasing me.

As I get close to the river, I see my brother hanging from a rope. His ankle is caught, and he is upside down. He is laughing as Anne stabs me in the back. As I'm lying there bleeding, I see a small girl rocking back and forth. She is sitting in a casket by the rocks. She is wearing all white, and her hair is red. I think she looks like an angel. Her long fingernails are jagged, and I realize she is not good. She is an evil child, like a bad Raggedy Ann doll. Her eyes are cut out in crisscrosses, just like Sarah's were. I look closer and see blood seeping out of her eyes. The casket door opens wide, and she grabs me and pulls me into it.

I wake up abruptly and look around to see if anyone has heard me. What is wrong with my mind? Why am I dreaming like this? I listen intently and hear nothing. Maybe I got lucky this time and made no sounds to alert anyone at the commune. I move around just a bit because my legs have fallen sleep. I look through my binoculars and see more followers who I used to go to church and eat with. They were not bad people. The commune takes in people when they have no other place to go.

Someone grabs my shoulder and puts their hand over my mouth. I scream, but no one hears me. My scream is muffled by their hand. I'm being dragged toward the small yellow car. I lose my sneakers, and my feet are hurting as they hit the rocks and dirt. I think my toes are bleeding. Who has me?

CHAPTER FOURTEEN
CAUGHT AGAIN

I wake up in a small building that was used for punishment when people did something very bad at the commune. It is called the "House of Isolation." I wouldn't even call it a building because it is so small. It is more like an outhouse. I had never seen the inside, but Cindy had to go there once for getting caught smoking marijuana. She told me all about her ordeal. She did not have anything to eat or drink for a whole week. I'm not sure how she survived. They had a small pot in the corner where she could urinate. She had to sleep on the floor with no blankets or pillows.

I can see the pot in the corner. I'm so scared. I've really screwed up again. I'm caught, and I don't know what to do. I'm in the hell-hole where Cindy was punished. She told me that she nearly died in there. Am I going to die?

Who found me?

I hear people talking outside. I hope they don't come inside and attack me. I can only imagine what my punishment will be. My feet are bleeding and aching badly. What will they do to me? Will they beat me again?

Leader Charles and Jerry are talking. Jerry is alive! A sense of relief comes over me, and I say a small prayer to God to thank him. I hope Cindy is alive. I pray that the police will find me soon. If I have to stay here, I will be put through some horrible times.

Leader Charles tells Jerry that I must have the ultimate punishment for what I have done. I've already gone through so many struggles, and I can't imagine what they will put me through this time. I was only trying to see if I was innocent of killing two people in the commune. I didn't want to go back, but they captured me. I wonder if these horrible men will give me a chance to explain why I was watching them. I needed to find out if I was a murderer. I hope someone will listen to me. I'm innocent, but in my heart, I know they will not believe me. I pissed them off when I ran away. They will do bad things to me.

Leader Charles says, "Jerry, what are we going to do with her? She has exposed us to the outside with all the rapes, beatings, and illegal abortions. I'm not sure if she knows about the other drugs, but she knows about the marijuana we grow and sell here. Cindy told her that when she was here. We have to get rid of her. Don't you agree? We have to do something before the authorities come for us. She is such a blabbermouth. I know she told everything."

Jerry says, "I'm not so sure she would tell the outsiders. She would be too embarrassed to say she was raped and beaten here. She is a fine Christian woman and telling them would make her an outcast in her community. I'm still in love with her, but I couldn't handle the holy terrors she would have at night. I don't want to get rid of her."

Leader Charles says, "You may be right about her not talking. I know how strong Christian people are. They are holier than thou. I'll only agree to keep her alive if we agree on her punishment. We will have to put her through extreme brainwashing. I guess that's what you would call it. If she is going to stay here, I don't want her to remember her past life or what happened to her at the commune. I can't believe you still like that stupid bitch. She has caused us so much grief.

"I've read about brainwashing techniques. We need to isolate her from everyone and not tell her what is going on. We will start a regimen requiring her to have absolute obedience and humility to us. We will reward her for the obedience but physically and psychologically punish her for noncooperation. We must destroy her loyalty to her family and friends by manipulating her thoughts. Right now, she is an unbeliever, and we must train her to have allegiance to us."

Jerry says, "OK, I'm willing to do anything to help with this process. I will take it upon myself personally to start it … with your permission, sir. I know a little about brainwashing. I experienced it once when I was younger. I've lived in many places and have had several bad things happen to me. It will be very painful for her at first, but I'm willing to go through the hard stuff so that she can live. We must deprive her of food and sleep. The bondage and torture will need to be started too. Is this OK with you, Leader Charles?"

"Yes, but we must be very careful to not get caught. What has she told her family and the outsiders? I know you said you didn't think she had talked to anyone due to being embarrassed, but we need to find out for sure. We need to hook her up to a lie detector machine and try to get every bit of information out of her. Do you hear me, Jerry? I want her to be a new woman for you. She must not remember anything from her past."

Jerry replies, "Yes, I hear you. After the lie detector, we will know what she knows about us and why she was spying on us. We will do the ultimate brainwashing that can be done to a person. I love her, and it will hurt to see her go through this, but I know it is required for her to stay here. I want her alive."

Leader Charles whispers, "Jerry, I will kill her if this doesn't work."

"I know you will, and I know you wouldn't do that unless you absolutely had to. Thank you, sir."

They walk away from my building. What idiots. I heard everything they said. Did they want me to hear it all—or are they that dumb? As I drift off to sleep, I have another dream.

I'm hiding behind a large tree, and I have my binoculars in my hands. I look down, and there is blood all over my hands. I raise the bloody binoculars to my eyes, and I see a man coming after me. It's Leader Charles, and he is extremely angry. Jerry is right behind him. They grab me and drag me over to the yellow car. I still have the binoculars, and I hit Leader Charles over the head with them. Jerry slaps me, and blood drips down my chin. Leader Charles pulls my arm so hard that I think it has been pulled out of its socket. I scream, "Why?" He just laughs in my face and tells me to handle it. He tells me that I am his harlot and that I belong to him. He walks over to a small case and grabs a whip and starts hitting me with it. He rips off my clothes and rapes me. I turn my face to the side so he cannot see the anguished look on it. I don't want him to see my tortured face. He laughs again and tells me it will get worse if I tell anyone.

I wake up and scream so loud that it echoes in the small box that I'm in. I'm shaking as I remember I've been captured by terrible men at the commune. I hope no one hears me as I have scream after that horrible dream. Leader Charles is Satan. Is it night or day? I can't tell. It is very dark in here. What is going to happen to me? Will they kill me? Will I ever get to see Gary, my babies, and my family again?

CHAPTER FIFTEEN
LISTENING

I'm going in and out of consciousness. I guess they drugged me to make me sleep most of the time. Maybe they think it will keep me from dreaming and screaming so the others won't hear me. My mind is thinking about what comes next. I wonder where they got a lie detector machine. I guess they stole it like they stole all the other things. I listen to every little thing that is going on outside. Because it is so dark here, I still don't know if it is day or night. I drift off to sleep again on the cold floor.

I'm sitting in a big hole that is full of leaves. My binoculars are broken. I wonder who broke them. Was it Leader Charles or Jerry when they captured me? I jump up and start running toward the House of Blood. Someone with a large shovel is chasing me, but I can't see their face. As they get closer, I feel their breath on the back of my neck. I turn around again, and blood is pouring out of Cindy's mouth. She is wearing the same bloody dress from the day I thought I stabbed her and Jerry.

She starts to hit me, and I wake up for a minute and then drift off again.

I'm being chased by wolves again. As I am running from them, I keep looking back to see how close they are. Saliva drips from their teeth If they catch me, I know they will start eating my flesh. I know they will kill me. I keep running away from them. I finally get to the river and jump in. For some reason, I don't think they will come into the water. I know I will be saved from them. I stay in the water, and the wolves stay on the riverbank. They are barking and growling at me. I climb out of the water and start stabbing something on the ground. Someone walks up behind me, and I look at them. It is Mama, and she is yelling at me to stop using her kitchen knives. I look to see what I am stabbing, and it is a toy mouse. It isn't even real. Mama jerks the knife out of my hand and takes off running. She is running toward our house. I look down and see that the toy mouse has turned into Harold. I have gotten everything that I wanted. I can have my Gary back now. I smile into Harold's empty eyes. They are gone.

As I whimper from my night terrors, I awake and hear a soft voice on the other side of my door.

"Please be quiet, Rachael. They will hear you." It is Cindy. She sounds good.

I reply, "Cindy, what are you wearing?"

"I'm wearing a bright skirt with a yellow shirt. Why?" Her voice sounds odd.

"Cindy, I had the most horrible dream about you. You had a bloody dress and a shovel, and you were going to kill me with it. I'm so glad you don't have that dress on."

"Girl, you're in a whole lot of trouble now. You escaped from the commune and stole my car. I guess my car belongs to the commune and is not mine any longer. I knew you would bring it back. I had faith in you. I knew you are a good girl."

"I'm not such a good girl now. I just wanted to find out if you and Jerry were alive. I'm in the isolation house, and I'm miserable. Every bone inside me hurts. I don't know if it's night or day. I'm so cold, my whole-body hurts, and I'm thirsty."

"Well, you will be sweating and freezing in here for a long time for running away like that and stealing our car."

"I'm sorry, Cindy. I promise I will never do it again. I promise I was just trying to investigate. I never told anyone about this place. I wanted to put all of that behind me. Besides, it isn't a bad place."

Cindy said, "I overheard people talking about the punishments that have happened here. Some of the followers said they will pull out your fingernails. Some said they will shave your head. I know it's all talk because only Leader Charles and Jerry know the plan for you. All I know is you are in big trouble, girl! You came back and got caught. It is all your fault. I've got to go. I'll see you later."

On the cold floor, I felt like a fool for getting caught. I was sneaky and didn't get caught when I was investigating Harold. I think of myself as a detective. I bet Officer Dale and Detective Joe would laugh at me for getting caught. They would not think I was very good at it. I guess they are right since I did get caught. I didn't even hear them sneaking up on me. I nearly jumped out of my skin when they grabbed my shoulder. I had no clue someone was about to get me.

As the medicine kicks in again, I drift off to sleep. What drugs did they give me? Is it making me dream more?

I look down at the knife in my hand. It has blood all over it. My other hand is holding a mouse. Harold is staring at me. Blood is pouring out of his stomach. What in the world am I doing with this knife? My brother is running toward Harold. Harold is laughing at him because Joe's zipper is undone. Harold is pointing and laughing. Joe punches him in the face and runs away. Harold grabs the mouse and stabs it with my knife. I start crying. I can't understand why he hurt that mouse. Harold pushes me down, and as I get up, he starts chasing me with a hammer. It is a bloody one, and I know, he will hit me in the head if he catches me. I will be dead. I run into a clown, and we jump on a Ferris wheel. We are both laughing at Harold as he is standing on the ground. The bar holding us in our seat breaks. I fall to the ground, and Harold grabs me. The hammer has been replaced with a knife in his bloody hands. I see the knife coming close to my throat as he slices me.

When I awake, I'm shaking all over. I'm so glad I didn't scream and let anyone outside hear me. They would beat me, especially Leader Charles. Does this dream mean that Joe might save me? I don't care who comes—I need to be saved. Oh, how I miss my family. What are they thinking? Are they freaking out with worry? What is ahead of me? I drift off into my dreams again.

Leader Charles and Jerry capture me and put me in a small box. I scratch the walls until my fingers bleed. Veronica, my sister, opens the door and tells me to get out. As I crawl out, she tells me that we have to run fast. As I am running beside her, I see Jerry chasing us. Veronica jumps on a brown horse and tells me to jump on the back. I grab her hand, and she lifts me onto the back of the horse. As we are about to be saved, someone grabs me and pulls me to the ground. As I hit the dirt, I start crying. I know I'm not going to be saved. I jump up and start running away, but can't see what or who it is. I just hear the sounds of their feet hitting the ground. I speed up and trip, landing on something very hard. It is the top of a casket. Who is in this casket? Where am I? As I look around, I realize I am in a cemetery, and it is very dark. The footsteps stop. I see my sister Veronica again and think, *Yay, I'm saved now.* She turns her head toward me, and her eyes are like the Raggedy Ann doll with the eyes cut out. She says nothing and just stares at me. I think, *How can she see with no eyes?* Behind her, there are wolves. The wolves want to eat me, but Veronica keeps them from getting me. She is protecting me again. She begins to laugh and tells me that she is the one who had scared me my whole life. She tells me that it was fun. I look at her face, and blood is rolling down it. I see the knife in her hand. She raises her hand.

When I wake up from this dream, I'm still in the horrible isolation box. I am crying, and I can feel the tears on my face. There is no Veronica or a horse to save me. Veronica is bad now. I feel so helpless, and I start praying. I have no one to help me but God. Dear God, please rescue me from this awful place that I have put myself in. I promise I will be good from now on and not investigate anything else. I promise to follow your ways, Jesus. I will feed the poor and help everyone. I promise … please help me. I finally drift off to sleep again.

Someone is trying to get me. Someone is always trying to get me. This seems to be my life's fear. I am being chased. It is Harold in my dream. As I slip and fall, I playacted like I can't get up. Harold comes closer to me, and I am able to hit his head with a large rock. As he is lying at my feet, I run and get a knife and start stabbing him from his head to his feet. I do this all the way up and down his body. He doesn't move, and as I am walking away, he grabs my ankle. I start running away again. I look behind me and see Jerry. He is chasing me, and Gary knocks him down. Gary starts beating his face. Jerry is laughing and starts telling Gary that I'm a whore. Gary begins to cut Jerry with a knife. It is my knife, and it is so bloody. I look down again and see a clown, not Jerry, with its eyes cut out. I run as fast as I can as someone is chasing me.

Oh, how I wish my night terrors would go away.

CHAPTER SIXTEEN
MISSING RACHAEL

Mama and Dad call Gary when I've been gone too long at my sleep study. I am normally gone for five or six hours. I pick up the boys around four o'clock and get home in time to make a good dinner for Gary. Gary gets home around five o'clock every day. I have my own *Leave It to Beaver* family now.

Mama calls Gary and says, "It's after five o'clock, and Rachael has not picked up the boys. Have you talked to her?"

Gary says, "I haven't heard from her. Wasn't she having a sleep study today? I think she goes to them at least once a week."

Mama says, "Yes, but I don't know exactly where she goes. She has never been this late before. I hope nothing has happened to her. She tends to get herself in trouble."

Gary says, "Let me call the therapist's office and ask where she goes for this procedure. I will call you back as soon as I hear anything."

Gary calls, but the office is closed for the day. He drives to the therapist's office and sees a man walking toward the parking lot. He jumps out of his car and runs up to the man. "Hello. Are you Spencer? I'm Rachael's husband, Gary Camper. Have you seen her today? She had some type of sleep study for her dreams and hasn't come home."

Spencer replies, "I haven't seen Rachael since last week. At our last session, she got upset with me, and I felt like she probably wasn't going to return."

Gary asks, "She has been missing all day, and I'm worried. Why did she get upset?"

Spencer says, "She got upset when I asked about the commune. I pushed her about it. She is so suspicious of me, and she accused me of being part of the commune."

Gary asks, "I need to find her quickly. She left our boys with her parents today. She told them she was going to have a sleep study test done today. She has done this before. Do you know where these sleep studies are done?"

Spencer says, "I don't know anything about a sleep study. I did not set her up for any tests. I'm her therapist, but I know she also sees a psychologist from time to time. However, they don't send patients for sleep studies either. I think she would have to be seeing a neurologist to get this set up, and they don't help with the prevention of dreams or night terrors. As far as I know, she is not doing any sleep studies."

Gary exclaims, "Oh, God, where is she?"

Spencer says, "After her session last week, she was mad at me. I didn't believe she would come back. I asked her to keep up the therapy and make an appointment for next week. I checked my appointments and didn't see one set up. I assumed she dropped me."

Gary asks, "Where do you think she is?"

Spencer says, "She talked so much about the commune. I think she may have gone back."

Gary says, "I'm going to the police department to report her missing. This is crazy. I can't lose my wife and the mother of my children again. I can't believe this is happening."

Spencer walks toward his car. "I'm going with you. Maybe I can help with the location of the commune. I'll follow you."

At the police station, Gary borrows their phone and calls Mama and Dad. He tells them about the therapist.

Mama and Dad tell him the kids can stay there.

Gary asks, "Can I talk to Officer Dale? My wife is missing, and he helped us before."

Gary is told to have a seat.

Officer Dale walks into the lobby and shakes Gary's hand. "What is going on with Rachael? Is she missing again? Come to my office."

Gary replies, "Officer, she has been missing since this morning. She left our kids with her parents and has been gone for eight hours. She told her parents she was going to a sleep study to help her with her dreams. Mama said she is usually gone four to six hours. She always picks them up by four o'clock, but she didn't come back today. I went to her therapist, Spencer, but he has no clue where she is. In fact, Spencer should be here any minute now. I think she stopped seeing him last week because she got suspicious of him being a part of the commune."

Spencer knocks on the door and sits down.

"Hi, Spencer. Do you think Rachael ran away? When was the last time you saw her? Did Rachael stop the weekly therapy with you? Are you aware of any sleep studies that she might be doing?"

Spencer replies, "Officer, so many questions. She has not said anything to me about stopping the therapy sessions or any sleep studies. I know that she was upset with me last week."

Officer Dale says, "Spencer, when was the last time you saw Rachael? Do you have any idea where she might be?"

Spencer says, "I saw her last week, and we discussed the commune. She got very upset with me and told me she didn't believe she needed the therapy classes any longer. I encouraged her to keep coming. She was very suspicious of me being a part of the commune and thought I was trying to trick her."

Officer Dale says, "I'm going to put out a bulletin for a missing woman. It's only been eight hours, but I know Rachael. I think she may be in trouble. Don't worry. We will find her soon."

Gary says, "Mama has probably put out an all-points bulletin, and all the townspeople will be looking for Rachael too. I know the whole town will turn out to try to find her. What if her car broke down? She took the yellow car. If she was returning it to the commune, she will be home soon."

Officer Dale says, "That's a possibility. I know our officers will find her. Gary don't be so worried. We will find your wife."

Spencer says, "What if she tries to go back to the commune? Will they be nice to her? She ran away from them once. I hope they are not mad at her."

Gary says, "I know she won't leave me and our boys again. What if someone got her? We have got to keep searching for her. Maybe she just needed to get away. I know her dreams are driving her crazy."

Officer Dale assures Gary and Spencer that they will find Rachael.

Gary heads over to Mama and Dad's house to get the boys.

CHAPTER SEVENTEEN
PUNISHMENT WOES

It's been about a week, and I'm still in the isolation building. The drugs have worn off, and I'm so thirsty. I'm too scared to cry out and ask for water or any kind of help. Cindy has not come back to talk to me. She's probably scared that she will get in trouble. I haven't heard Leader Charles or Jerry. I think they are letting me sweat for a while, worrying about what's going to happen to me. I'm not sure how much longer I can go on. I'm so tired, weak, and thirsty. I can hardly raise my head up off the floor. Do I really want them to get me out of here? What is next for me?

I'm hallucinating and seeing things on the walls. I think I see a spider, and I need to catch it and eat it. I need something in my stomach. I don't have to use the small container to pee in because I don't need to pee at all at this point. I haven't had anything to drink in so long. I realize it's not the spider I'm seeing; it may be a mouse. At this point, I am really seeing things. Is that a rainbow above my head on the ceiling? I think it may be because I'm so close to death that I might be seeing part of heaven.

The door opens, and the light comes in. I can hardly see for a minute. It's Mama and Dad and James and John. I'm so glad to see them. Leader Charles is behind them. He pushes them into the small area with me and shuts the door. My family is now captured too. What is going on here? I'm confused. I start screaming my head off as I am running away from someone. I look back and see Joe. My brother is laughing at me and yelling, "You're a scaredy-cat!" I reach the river, and all my friends are floating in the river. They are not playing or splashing in the water. They are all dead in pools of blood and water. Joe screams, "You did this!" Then, Harold starts stabbing himself.

I wake up again and realize I was dreaming or hallucinating. The door opens slowly, and it is Leader Charles and Jerry. Jerry grabs my arm and stands me up. He gives me a small glass of water. I'm so thankful, but all I can do is drink it as fast as I can. I'm so weak, and I can hardly stand. The sunlight is blinding.

Jerry says, "I hear you are still having those horrible dreams that I hated so much the last time you were here. Why is this still going on? I thought you would be over the nightmares by now. What is wrong with you?"

Leader Charles says, "Rachael, we are taking you to a private place for a lie detector test. I want to know how much you know and what you have told the outsiders. This will not hurt you, but I will hurt you if you try to escape again."

I reply, "Yes, sir. I understand. I wanted to see if Jerry and Cindy were still alive. I didn't want to be captured. If you let me go, I promise not to say a word."

Leader Charles stares at me with hatred in his eyes.

Jerry says, "We're going to my car, and I will blindfold you. You will not be able to know where we are going. We are going to get to the bottom of everything you know about our commune. I promise we will not hurt you unless you do something stupid. Do you hear me, girl?"

I say, "Yes, Jerry. I understand. I can't walk very well right now. Can I have more water and maybe some crackers?"

Leader Charles says, "You don't deserve anything right now. For all I care, you can die. You have crossed us for the last time."

As we are walking toward the car, I see the followers staring at me. I guess I'm the black sheep of the family now. Jerry shoves me into the back seat with him, and Leader Charles is driving. They blindfold me, and I can't see where they are taking me. I am so worried about where we are going. I also worry about my family. What are they thinking? I know Gary is going out of his mind with worry about me. I hope he talks to Spencer and Officer Dale. Maybe Spencer will remember where the commune is, and they can put two and two together and find me.

I think about the lie detector test. If I lie, they will be able to tell. I decide to be honest and tell the truth. I don't want to go back to that isolation box. I'm not sure if they will put me back in there anyway. What have I gotten myself into? I know things will be worse for me this time around. I know they are all mad at me.

After about two hours, the car stops. I'm so afraid that I'm going to say something I shouldn't say during the lie detector test. I think about Gary, my sons, and my family. I know they are going crazy since I didn't come home. I hope they have gone to the authorities to tell them that I've been kidnapped. I hope they don't think I ran away again.

Jerry says, "You better not try to escape because it will be bad for you. Leader Charles wants to kill you. Remember the beatings and rapes from Leader Charles? It will be much worse this time around if you do anything or try to get away. You need to thank me that you're still alive."

I reply weakly, "Yes."

Leader Charles says, "We are here, and I don't want any funny business going on. Do not talk to anyone—not even the man who is questioning you. You will only talk when he asks you a question, and that is all. Do you hear me?"

I reply, "Yes, sir."

A door opens, and Jerry takes my hand. As I get out of the car, still blindfolded, I hear many cars traveling up and down the street. Are we near a highway? Jerry is guiding me as I walk. Even though they have given me water and crackers, I'm still so weak. My legs are wobbly, and Jerry has to support me as I walk.

I hear a door open, and a man tells Leader Charles and Jerry to come in. As I hear the door shut, Jerry takes off my blindfold. I'm in a nice house, but I have no clue where it is. I can still hear the cars going up and down the street. I try to take in all the details of my whereabouts. I see a window in the front room, but it is covered with a green curtain. I can see a brown house with yellow shutters across the street. I must remember this in case I need to come back here. I hope someone will rescue me.

CHAPTER EIGHTEEN
DETECTING NOTHING

I hear all three of the men talking and whispering about me. I can't understand what they are saying. I keep staring at the man so that I can identify him later. I'm sure he is a crook since he has a lie detector machine. He couldn't be a good guy doing this sort of thing. He probably stole the machine from the police. He looks like a creep and is so slimy. He looks like a weasel.

Leader Charles take money out of his wallet and hands it to the man. He unfolds a piece of paper and hands it to the man. I assume it's the questions they want him to ask me.

Leader Charles shakes the man's hand and says, "Thanks for doing this, Ernie. We want the truth about all the questions on this paper."

Ernie replies, "I'll do my best. The machine will not lie. It will detect her heart rate going crazy if she is lying about something."

Jerry says, "That's cool! I wish we had one of these at the commune. It would help when we think a follower is messing up or lying to us."

Leader Charles replies, "Let's get started on this. It's a long drive back. I'm not too thrilled driving on big highways in this area."

Ernie replies, "Yes, San Antonio is a very busy place."

Leader Charles turns to me and says, "Little girl, it's time to tell the truth. We have to know what you have told the outsiders. We don't want them finding us and shutting down our commune. We are a good place, and we are helping so many people. Do you hear me?"

I reply, "Yes, sir."

The man grabs my arm and leads me to a bedroom. I try to memorize everything I see. I see newspapers on the floor.

I sit in a chair, and Ernie hooks me up to a machine. It looks like they are going to do an EKG on me. I'm so scared, but he is not hurting me. He turns on his machine, and it makes a buzzing noise. He sits down near the machine and grabs the paper.

I bet this sleazy man is a crook—just like Leader Charles and Jerry. I've got to play it cool and not let my blood pressure go up. I remain as calm as I can be. I tell myself that I need to think about my family and what a joy they are to me. I love all of them so much, but I have screwed up things again. As it is about to start, I take a big breath and let it out.

Ernie says, "Here's the first question for you, young lady: Where do you live?"

I reply, "I live in a Carrizo Springs, Texas."

"Good. Who are your mother and father?"

"My father's name is Howard Chaney, and my mother's name is Irene Chaney."

"Are you married?"

I reply, "Yes, I am legally married to a man named Gary. I'm also married to Jerry—he is right here—but I don't think it is legal.

Maybe it is to him 'in the eyes of the Lord' but it's not to me. He is a sweet man, and we were married at the commune."

Ernie seemed satisfied with my answers so far. He says, "Rachael, do you know where this commune is?"

I say, "Yes. Cindy told me it is near Laredo, Texas. I don't know the names of the roads out to the commune, but I found it. These bad men captured me. Please help me."

He ignores my cry for help. "Did you tell anyone where you were going?"

"No, I did not. I left my boys with my parents and told them I would be gone all day for a sleep study. I have night terrors that I can't stop. They believed me because they want me to get help."

Ernie says, "Just answer my questions. Don't add all this extra garbage about your issues. I'm here to get the truth out of you."

I reply, "Yes, sir."

"Are you going to try to escape again?"

I try to be as truthful as I can be. "I'm not sure. If I get a chance, I will try to get back to my family. I have twin babies, two of them. Both of them are boys. The people at the commune are all brainwashed and do whatever these evil men tell them to do. For all I know, they will eventually make us drink spiked Kool-Aid."

Ernie replies, "You do what you are told, and nothing will happen to you. Just shut up and answer the questions. Do you know the legal names of anyone at the commune?"

"No, I do not."

"Did Cindy tell you any legal names of any people at the commune?"

"I can't remember if she did."

"Do you know who Leader Charles is? Did you investigate who he was?"

"No, I did not."

The questions continued, and I answered them as best I could. My heart rate must have gone up when I lied about certain things.

I do know that Leader Charles moved to Texas from Utah. He is a crook and seeks out weak people to control and follow him. He thinks he is part of the trinity—or that's what he makes the followers believe. He is a control freak and makes the followers worship him. In my heart, I'm scared of him—and I don't want to be beaten and raped again.

After a couple of hours, he tells me that he is done. He unstraps me from all of the wires and leads me back to the living room.

Leader Charles and Jerry are surrounded by fast-food wrappers. It looks like they came from DQ. I have to remember that if I ever get away again. I'm very proud of myself for remembering little things that could help in an investigation. I probably need to go to school, just like Joe did, and become a detective. I think Ernie is a crook and needs to be caught. He shouldn't be doing these types of illegal things for evil people. However, I know it's just work to him. He is just earning a buck.

I'm blindfolded again as we return to the commune. It's a long ride, and I'm still tired, thirsty, and hungry. So much for hoping as they place me back into the House of Isolation. The floor is hard and uncomfortable. It's OK during the day, but it gets very cold at night. I am miserable and have really messed up my life again. Of course, these people have no mercy on me. I wonder how much longer it will last.

I start dreaming that I'm tied down to a table, and wires are tied all around me. A face is staring down at me. It is the face of a psychopath. It is the serial killer, Harold. He takes a knife and slices my legs from the knees to the ankles. He is smiling as if he is enjoying every moment. I start screaming from the pain, but he just laughs at me. I know I need stitches. Then, someone is chasing me through the woods with a knife. I am so scared, and I keep running as fast as

I can. I trip and fall and am terrified. As I turn around, I see a hairy figure coming toward me. I had always heard of Bigfoot. I think, *This is it. It's going to kill me.* I disappear. I walk down an aisle and enter a building with a large cross on it. I walk down the aisle and see Harold. Harold has a knife, and he stabs Ryan and Sarah in the eyes again. He turns around and stares at me and starts laughing. That's when I see Gary, James, and John with Harold. He has them down by the water. Bigfoot reappears down by the river. Someone is chasing me. I am running as fast as I can. Is it Harold or Bigfoot coming after me?

Loud screams come out of me. I am terrified and want to go home so badly. Will this nightmare ever be over?

CHAPTER NINETEEN
OUT OF THE BOX

After a few more days, they open the door again. The sunlight hurts my eyes, and my legs are still very weak.

Leader Charles and Jerry walk me to a building that I've never seen. I can't believe I can even walk. The building looks very new, and I realize it is one of the buildings they were working on when I was there the last time. Is this the House of Torture?

I remember overhearing them saying that I must be brainwashed. I wonder what is going to happen to me. I wonder how someone is brainwashed. The followers are not in their right minds. They can't all be here of their own will. Folks here are running from various troubles in their lives. They usually move on after a while. I don't think all of them like to be told what to do.

I look around the grounds and see a few people I recognize. No one waves at me or even looks up. I figure they would all be staring at me for escaping and then getting captured again. Everyone knows that I ran away, and everyone knows I'm in trouble now.

As we walk in front of the canteen, I see Cook standing there. She does not even act like she knows me. I guess she doesn't want to get in trouble. She knows I'm in trouble. She always told me to do what I'm told, and then I wouldn't get in trouble. Cook used to like me, but now she doesn't. She probably thinks I'm a fool. I guess Cook likes it here at the commune, and she is grateful to get to live here. I wonder what brought Cook here at this commune. She seems to like it very much.

As we enter this building, I see all types of tables and chairs. There is one bed in the room, and they lead me to it. I sit on the side of the bed and stare at my surroundings. I wonder what the name of this new building is.

Leader Charles says, "Lay down and rest because you're not going to get any for quite a while. Tomorrow is a different day for you. Do not fight us on this—or it will go worse for you."

Jerry says, "Rachael, obey—and you will be fine. Don't fight this. You can't stop it. You won't die."

They walk out the door and lock it behind them. I fall asleep on the bed immediately.

I'm running from something, but I can't figure out what or who they are. I look again, and I see a mean-looking man with cowboy boots on. His beady eyes look like they have blood in them. It is the same man in my dream where Mama and I were putting away groceries. He has a hose in his hand, and the water is running. He grabs me, holds me down, and squirts water in my face. I can't breathe and start fighting him. He grabs a towel, puts it on my face, and continues to put the water on my face. I am screaming and flailing my arms. I think I'm drowning. He hits me, and I go to sleep. All of a sudden, I catch an unknown man and make him lay down on the ground in the woods beside the river. Maybe he is a homeless person.

I didn't know him. I take a knife with a blade that is very unusual and sharp. It has a tip on one end, and it is very wide and angled down. I calmly start stabbing him from his left foot all the way up to his head. I then stab him from his right foot up to his head. The man doesn't scream as I am stabbing him. I show no emotion, and it feels like I am in a trance. I then quit stabbing him. Is this Harold that I am killing?

When I wake up, I realize it was just a dream. Is this what they are going to do to me next? Or am I going to end up being the killer? I think about Gary and James and John, and I hope they never find out what they do to me. Oh, I miss them. Why in the world did I think I needed to investigate? I wanted to find out if Jerry and Cindy were still alive. I didn't want to get captured. I guess I wasn't careful enough.

I'm back at the commune. I think about all the things that happened when I was here. I remember some good things, but I mostly remember the beatings and rapes. They were mostly done by Leader Charles, but Jerry did them too. I thought Jerry loved me. Those men are capable of anything—possibly even murder.

I try to figure out what they named the new building. It's got to be something horrible. Maybe it's something about pain and torture.

I'm so scared, but I eventually drift off to sleep.

I wake up and realize I'm in the House of Torture. Chains and whips are everywhere. Scary animal heads hang on the walls. They look like they are going to jump on me and kill me. I look over and see my sister Veronica. She is laughing and playing with a clown doll. She likes dolls so much. Veronica throws the doll on the floor and runs over to me. She says, "They are going to get you, Rachael. I will save you though." She jumps up and runs out of the room. I then see that I'm at the wedding of Veronica. I see what she is wearing, and I laugh. She is wearing white shorts and a lacy blouse with suspenders. Her soon-to-be husband is wearing a matching outfit, but he had long white pants instead of shorts. They both put on brown leather coats. I don't know who her husband is, but he is very upset because the food has not arrived. When the food arrives, there is blood all over it. I look around search for someone with a knife. I see Harold, and he has cut someone's eyes out. Blood is gushing onto the food. Harold turns around and faces me. I turn around and run.

I awaken suddenly from that awful dream and am shaking all over. I am so confused about how Veronica is tied into all of this. I think, *Is she a good sister or a bad sister?*

Cook is in this house with me. She brings me toast and a small cup of coffee. She doesn't say a word as I walk over to a table and sit down.

Cook looks at me sternly and says, "Rachael, I can't talk to you. I have strict orders."

I reply, "I know you can't talk to me, but you can help me. I'm sorry I came here again. I was just trying to find out if I had murdered Jerry and Cindy."

Cook replies, "Of course you didn't kill anyone. I even know that about you."

"I didn't know for sure. I have these awful dreams, and I don't know reality from the things in my head."

"I told you to obey all the rules and stay out of trouble. You're in a bad situation now!"

"Cook, please help me. What are they going to do to me? I should have obeyed all the rules around here."

Cook says, "I can't help you. I would get in trouble. What would you want me to do anyway? This is all I will be saying to you. I don't want to disobey any orders. Please do what they say from now on."

I reply, "I understand. Thank you for the breakfast."

As Cook leaves the building, Leader Charles and Jerry enter. They look at Cook with approval on their faces.

CHAPTER TWENTY
BRAINWASHING SAGA

Leader Charles and Jerry change their expressions immediately. They look evil and angry. What are they going to do to me? They grab my arms.

I try to fight them, but it does no good. Jerry injects a needle into my arm. I wonder what they are giving me. My mind is getting hazy. They lead me over to a table and lay me down on it. It is so cold and hard on my back. I want them to have mercy on me, but I know they will not give me any mercy.

Leader Charles says, "Jerry, I think the injection is working. She seems very out of it. I've heard that the lasting effects of our treatments depend on the personalities of the individuals. The degree of persuasion and the attitude process we use must be very strong to be effective. She is so strong, and I'm sick of her."

As I'm drifting off, Jerry says, "Are you ready for me to start the movie?"

Leader Charles replies, "Yes, start it now. We will leave and let her wake up slowly. She will watch it over and over for the rest of the day."

Jerry replies, "Yes, she definitely needs an attitude change. I certainly hope this psychological movie will subconsciously lead her in the right direction by using the mode of suggestion process. It should put some ideas in her head that our commune is a good place—and this is where she belongs. I certainly hope so."

Leader Charles says, "For sure, she needs to lose her identity, become one of us, and forget her old life. I can't believe she came back here. If she is to remain with you, she will need some tough treatment. Just because she has interrupted our lives again, it doesn't mean we have to stop our ways. Let's start the movie, and then we have to go tend to some things."

Jerry replies, "Rachael, this better work. Otherwise, I won't be responsible for what happens to you."

I'm so groggy as I start waking up. My arms and legs are tied down, and there is a movie on a large screen. I start watching it, but I'm still very drowsy and dazed. What did they inject in my arm? I think they are hypnotizing me with the drugs and then showing me all types of weird shapes and sounds. I believe they are trying to manipulate my mind into believing the commune is where I belong. Are they trying to traumatize me because being tied down for this long is really messing with my mind? The medicine is making me go in and out of consciousness. I feel like I'm floating on air. I continue watching the shapes. Will they ever stop?

I keep waking up and going back to sleep. At some point, I have an awful dream.

I'm standing near the river, and Jerry comes toward me with a rope. He places it around my neck and starts tightening it. Spencer is laughing at me. He and Veronica have blood all over their clothes. Are they dead? They laugh harder when Jerry tightens the rope again. It is so tight, and my tongue is hanging out. Veronica grabs my hand, and we run to the river. Where has the rope gone? We jump on a float and start having fun. A large rat starts chasing me out of the river. I run to our church and start praying on the front steps. As I sit on the steps, I look at the rat. It stops running and is watching me. His eyes are black, and his teeth are very large. I am shaking. I know this rat is going to get me. Harold, jumps out, grabs the rat, and runs off with it. I see a figure in the dark. It is just standing there and watching me. I stare so hard and try to make out who he is. I don't move. I am afraid he will kill me. I know he is going to grab me. He starts walking toward me. I can see his face, and it has wicked scars all over it. It looks like someone sliced his face with a knife. I realize it is Spencer as he reaches out and grabs me.

I wake up confused and shaken. There was a rope around my neck, and then it was gone. I'm so confused about this dream. Why did Spencer and Veronica have blood on them? I love my sister so much. She has always protected me during my horrible dreams. Spencer was the nerd I used to see in therapy, but I suspected him of being involved with the commune. I look around and remember the mess I've gotten myself into. Why do I do these things?

Jerry enters the building, turns off the movie, and unstraps me. He picks me up, puts me back in bed, and pats me on the shoulder. Maybe Jerry does love me.

Cook enters the building and leaves some crackers and tea on the table. She leaves quietly without saying a word.

Jerry says, "Eat, Rachael. Tomorrow is a new day."

When he leaves, I wonder what is in store for me tomorrow. What comes next for me? They are starving me with only toast and crackers. What's the purpose of no food? I realize this is part of the process. I think about the movie and all the shapes and weird sounds. They are already getting into my head. When I watch it, I am in a trance.

I think about Gary, John, and James. I don't want to forget my family. I know they want me to forget my other life so I will not want to run away again. I know my family is extremely upset and worried about me. Gary is probably going out of his mind. I know Mama is crying so much and panicking. Dad is probably trying to stay calm. I hope they called the police and got Officer Dale to help. I know Joe is on top of things. I hope they don't think I ran away again.

As I think about my situation, I drift off to sleep.

Jerry is kissing Cindy right in front of me. I'm so mad at them, and I grab my knife to kill them. A clown crawls out from under the bed. I turn my eyes toward it as he is coming toward me. His eyes are bloodshot, and he has blood dripping from his long nails. He has a yellow wig on, and his face is painted green and red. He smiles at me, and there is blood dripping from his teeth. He is still crawling toward me, and then he grabs my ankles. I stab the clown with my knife.

I scream so loud that I feel the walls shaking. Why am I so jealous of Cindy and Jerry? They are in my dreams, and it's driving me crazy. As far as that scary clown, what in the world is that? I thought clowns were supposed to be fun. Don't children love them at their birthday parties? This one was so scary.

I am not able to go back to sleep, and I think about my life. What is going to happen to me? I know they want me to forget my old life and live in this commune forever. Will I ever be free again?

So much for all the medication I was taking. No more happy pills and pills to keep me from dreaming so much. I am on my own now, and I have to make the best of things. I hope I will be able to control my nightmares. I need to keep thinking happy thoughts. I don't know what's ahead of me. This is so terrible.

CHAPTER TWENTY-ONE

WILL IT EVER STOP?

Weeks go on, and every day, I'm placed on the table and strapped down by Jerry or Leader Charles. Jerry is nicer to me than Leader Charles. I know he hates me, and I have caused them troubles again. It is so cold and hard, and my body aches. After a while, I stop fighting them. I'm not injected with any drugs, but I still watch the crazy movies all day. Most of them are extremely hypnotic and put me into a trance. I've been like a zombie for a long time.

Leader Charles comes into the room with Jerry, and I hear them talking. I don't understand what they are saying at first. They sound like the Charlie Brown movie where all the adults are mumbling in the background.

Then I hear Leader Charles saying, "These movies are designed to slowly push aside the analytical part of her mind. I think they are great, and she will lose her memory soon. She will not be able to analyze or figure out how to escape. These movies are designed to make her believe whatever we tell her. She is being hypnotized permanently."

Jerry says, "I think it is a cool process. I'm glad you understand it, and I sure hope it works on her. I love her and want her to be mine again."

Leader Charles says, "I don't care about that, but that would be good for you. I want her to forget everything and start over as a new person. I don't want my commune shut down by the authorities, and I don't want to be arrested. I never want to go back to prison. It's not fun in there."

On the table today, I try to remember my family and my old life. My husband's name is Gary, and my boy's names are John and James. I know Mama and Dad are very upset. I have two sisters and a brother. I can't forget my family. I drift off to sleep again, but the movie keeps going. I wonder if it will ever stop.

All of a sudden, the door opens. Jerry enters quietly and changes the movie. He doesn't say a word to me. I turn my head toward him as he nears the front door, and he turns around and looks at me. He has no remorse on his face, and I don't feel like he is going to have mercy on me or help me at all.

I'm watching a reality show about being at a commune and the happiness that is there. The people are so happy, and everything seems so real. I hear them talking about their daily lives and what they are going to do that day. The movie is about two hours long, and as soon as it is over, it starts all over again. I watch it over and over. I try to think about my family, but my memory is fading quickly. My husband's name is Gary, and I have two boys. What are their names? I can't remember. I need to remember this, but things are starting to get mixed up in my head. Where do I live? How did I get on this table?

I think I've been in this building for at least two weeks. Every day, I'm given crackers and tea or water. Someone comes in and places me on this table. I have calluses on my wrists and ankles from being tied down every day.

I'm watching the commune happy movie again. I've memorized every word of it. What are they doing to me? My husband is Gary, and my baby boy's names are something I can't remember. I start crying again. My mind is slowly fading. I have a mother and father, but I don't remember their names. Their faces are fading in my mind. I start concentrating on my movie again. This commune is such a happy place. I hope I get to live in one. Everyone is so happy, and it must be wonderful to get to be there with all the happy followers. I drift off to sleep.

Spencer is helping Leader Charles and Jerry drag me through the woods. Where are they taking me? What did Spencer tell them? I knew he was part of the bad people when I was in counseling with him. When I look into Spencer's eyes, I see evil in them. He has blood all over his hands as he touches my face. He grabs my hair and pulls it so hard that I think he has pulled it out. He laughs as I scream. I am sitting in my room at home. My back is to the door. I keep hearing things behind me. I keep looking back to see if anyone is there. I think I hear a mouse in the wall as it is scratching sound. I then realize there is something on our roof. I walk outside and look at our roof. Spencer is hanging from a tree. His eyes are bugged out, and the wind is moving him back and forth. He is scraping against the roof. Blood is running out of his nose. This is what I have been hearing. My heart is beating so hard as I wake up.

I wake up shaking with fear, and the movie is still going. I dreamed about Spencer. He is the therapist I used to see. I'm convinced that he helped them capture me, and I don't trust him. He was probably mad at me for not showing up for my last session. He could have followed me and let the commune people know exactly where I was hiding. I'm not 100 percent sure, but I believe Spencer is my enemy.

I turn my attention back to the movie. I say the words to the movie aloud. I think being vocal might help my memory. I need to remember my boys' names. What are they? Mama's name is Irene something. I don't remember Dad's name at this point. I have two sisters and one brother, but I can't remember their names.

What am I watching on the screen? Why is it making me lose my memory? Is this how the brain works? What happens when people get Alzheimer's? My brain is so foggy, and my train of thought is completely lost. It's very hard to remember where I am. The table is so hard, and it is hurting my back.

Jerry walks into the building and stares at me.

I open my eyes and turn to him with pleading eyes.

"Rachael, you shouldn't have returned to this commune. It's too late now, and you have to endure this process. You will soon not remember any of your past. All you will remember is us and living here at this commune. It is a good place to live, and you must like it since you came back. If you run away again, you will be killed by Leader Charles. He has no mercy in his heart for you. He feels that you have been a nuisance here and have caused problems for the commune and all the followers. Just hang in there—and we will be finished at some point. You will live and not die."

I don't say a word as he leaves. I'm glad he is nice to me. Maybe I'll have a chance to live.

CHAPTER TWENTY-TWO

THE HOUSE OF TORTURE

I've been watching movies for about three weeks now, tied to a table, in the House of Torture. I made up three weeks since I really don't know how long I've been captured. I don't think they named this building the House of Torture, but that's what it is. I'm not actually being tortured physically, but they are driving me crazy. I'm losing my memory of my old life.

Leader Charles and Jerry have not moved me to the table yet. I get up weakly and start walking around and around. I need to maintain my strength in case I am rescued. My mind is foggy, but I still remember that I need to get away from this place. It is so evil in here, and I'm being brainwashed.

Cook enters my building, and I'm glad they are giving me more than just toast and crackers. I'm thankful because I have been losing so much weight. She brings me toast, scrambled eggs, bacon, and coffee. Some days, she brings me oatmeal and bacon. I always enjoy the coffee so much. It gives me the energy to exercise.

"Rachael, Leader Charles has informed me that I can talk to you—but only about the commune. This is a good place to live, and you are one of us now. You must never try to leave. Living here is great. You are lucky to be here. The followers and I love being here, and Leader Charles and Jerry are doing the best for us. They love us. We have nowhere else to go."

"I know, Cook. I kind of remember that I have other people who love me too. My brain is so foggy."

"I know, honey, but this commune is the best place to live—and so many people love you here too. You need to forget that old life. It was gone the minute you went nosing around here again and got captured."

I whisper, "I guess so."

Leader Charles and Jerry walk inside and give her a look of approval as she leaves. As the door shuts, they turn their attention to me.

Leader Charles says, "Rachael, we are going to change things up today. Do not fight us. Do you hear me?"

I reply, "Yes, sir."

He says, "You will be going through a type of asphyxiation where you will think you are dying, but you will be awakened before you die. This type of process will always be in the back of your mind that if you forsake us, you will die. You must feel this method of dying without really dying. Are you ready?"

I say, "Jerry, don't let him do this to me. Please help me."

Leader Charles says, "Don't ask Jerry. He has no control over this. You brought this on yourself, and now you have to take whatever we hand you. Jerry, bring Rachael to the table and tie her down."

Jerry does what he is asked, and I try to fight him. Jerry slaps me and picks me up.

Leader Charles straps me down.

Jerry says, "Rachael, you have to be still. We have the potential to kill you in this process."

I say, "Jerry, help me. Don't let him do this to me. Help me!"

Leader Charles takes a long strap and ties it around my neck. I feel it tightening, and my air supply is cut off. Didn't I dream about this the other night? I know they put a rope around my neck, but it's really happening now. I am being deprived of oxygen, and I'm losing consciousness.

I wake up and feel myself having a seizure. I'm shaking uncontrollably, but I finally calm down. They start the process again, and I'm being choked again. I gag and feel like I'm going to throw up. They roll me over, and I vomit. The choking continues. I feel tingling in my hands and feet and then nothing.

Leader Charles says, "Jerry, we will be doing this every morning after breakfast. Hopefully, the lack of oxygen to her brain will cause memory loss. There's a possibility of putting her into a coma, but I was told that she would eventually wake up."

The movie with the shapes and sounds is turned back on. I watch it from the table. How much more can I take? They will be back to do this every day? Who are these monsters? What are they doing to my brain? I think about my babies and how much fun I had playing with them. I may not remember their names, but I remember that I have kids. My husband's name is Gary—thank God I can still remember his name.

I pray all the time that I can keep my sanity. My memory is fading quickly, and just about all I can remember is this place and how mean Leader Charles is. Jerry is just a follower who will do anything the leader tells him to do. I can't wait until this ordeal is over. Will it ever end?

When evening arrives, I'm put back in my bed. I'm just worn out from going through the torture all day long. I know I've got to be a strong person to survive this. I know it's not going to be a good night. What will I dream about after the ordeal I went through today?

I'm running away from the commune, and Cindy and Jerry are chasing me. Their clothes are bloody. Jerry has a knife in one hand and a rat in the other one. Is he going to kill the rat—or me? As they get closer, I scream. My brother is on the ground with his head cut off. His body is just a bit away from his head.

Veronica runs up to me and grabs my hand, and we run away to an amusement park. We are walking toward a ride, and then a man comes over to us. His eyes are cut out, and purple blood is pouring out of them. Veronica laughs at him and goes over to a river that is running through the park. I have never seen this river. I'm frozen and can't move as I watch the blood dissolving into the water. Veronica is not scared of the blood or anything else. The man walks away from me, and I run over to Veronica. We jump into the river and start swimming. She acts like nothing happened. I'm just swimming and swimming in the river with blood all around me.

I wake up and am shaking all over. I keep replaying the dream in my mind. Veronica is always there, saving me as normal. I'm so glad it's a dream because I don't want my brother to be dead. Maybe the dream means that Veronica and Joe are going to save me. I sure hope Joe doesn't get killed while saving me.

I hear the door opening, and Cook brings in my breakfast. I get out of bed and wash my face. As I sit down to eat, I remember that I threw up all my food yesterday during the strangling process. Leader Charles is the devil. I believe he really wants me to die. He puts me near it and then resuscitates me for Jerry's sake. I'm a walking dead person. I guess I'm lucky that Jerry loves me and prevents Leader Charles from doing me in.

I say, "I believe I will wait to eat until later. I couldn't keep my food down yesterday."

As Cook leaves the building, she smiles at me.

CHAPTER TWENTY-THREE
TORTUROUS MEMORIES

Leader Charles and Jerry place me on the table and strap down my wrists and ankles. I try to fight them, but Leader Charles just cusses me and slaps me around. They begin the process of asphyxiation again. They choke me, and then I wake up. This is repeated several times. Leader Charles shows no remorse in what he is doing to me. I think I'm dying slowly.

I look at Jerry's face to see if he knows that they are torturing me almost to death. Does he have any remorse? I want to see if he is sorry for what they are doing to me. I can't tell for sure, but I think Jerry is nervous every time they repeat this process. Does Jerry think I might die each time?

As they leave, I doubt I'm going to live through this horrible torture. They return the next day and do it all over again. I think it has been about a week or so of this holy terror. The only thing different is they are letting me eat before they strap me down to start my day of movies. I guess they don't want to be vomited on.

I try to remember my family and anything about my old life. This torture has been going on for weeks. I've been through so much: strapped down, forced to watch happy and confusing movies, and choked to the point of losing consciousness. My old life is fading fast. My brain is not working like it used to. Are they killing my brain cells? What are they going to do to me next? I will find out tomorrow.

Cook does not show up the next morning. I think I've been in this building for about a month. Just when I think things can't get any worse, Leader Charles walks into the door, rips off my gown, and starts to rape me. After he is done sexually assaulting me, he throws me onto the floor and starts punching, slapping, and kicking me. He takes an iron rod and beats the soles of my feet. It hurts so much, and I scream in pain. The pain is excruciating. I don't think he will ever stop.

He is getting fully aroused as he hits me. He rapes me again, and I think I'm going to die. Tears are rolling down my face. He slaps me and tells me to quit crying because it won't help. After he climaxes again, he gets dressed and walks out. He did not say one word to me except to quit crying. He doesn't appear to feel sorry for me as he tortures me.

I try to breathe. I make myself get up and wash the blood off my body. My lips are bleeding and swollen. My eyes are turning purple. Will I be able to live through this torture? Why have the rapes and beatings started?

The next morning, it starts all over again. Leader Charles and Jerry choke me on the table, and I lose consciousness. I look at Jerry's face to see if he has any reaction to my badly beaten body. I know he sees my black eyes and my swollen lips. I can feel the dried blood on them. Jerry shows no remorse in front of Leader Charles.

As Leader Charles and Jerry leave, Cook brings me some food.

My feet are so sensitive as I walk over to the table. I hope I do not get an infection.

Cook leaves the food on the table and walks back to the door. "Rachael, stay strong."

I reply, "I will."

Jerry returns, places me on the tables, and straps me down. He turns on the weird movies and leaves. My memory is fading fast. What will happen to me? Will I live in this commune forever?

As Jerry walks out, he says, "Rachael, you shouldn't have come back."

I reply, "I know. I keep getting myself into all kinds of trouble every time I come here. When will I learn my lesson?"

That night, Leader Charles removes me from the table and pushes me onto the bed. He rips off my gown and rapes me. I can see joy on his face as he climaxes. I wonder why he has refrained from beating me. I guess he thinks he could kill me if he gets ahold of me again. He leaves quickly.

I think something horrible. He may get me pregnant since I'm not on birth control. I hope the good Lord will keep that from happening. I wonder if Jerry knows that Leader Charles has been raping me. I don't think he cares; Jerry is such a weak person. I think Jerry is a follower and does not have one thought of his own. Will Jerry be next—or does Leader Charles want to control me all by himself?

Cook brings me food, looks at me, and shakes her head. "Rachael, when are you going to learn your lesson? This place is a good place to live unless you do something to make the leaders mad. I'm going to tell you some things, but you must never repeat them, OK?"

I reply, "I promise I won't say a word. I'm just glad you are talking to me,"

"I've been here for a long time … maybe ten years or so. At first, I came here because I had nowhere else to go. My parents were both drug addicts, and my home life was horrible. I never knew who would be at our house. There were all types of bad people inside and out. When I was about years old, my father would let the men touch my privates. All of them would laugh at me. When I was twelve, my father started using me to make money. I would let men have sex with me, and they would give my dad money. I couldn't do anything about it. For years, I made money for my parents to live on. They even used my younger brother with the men who preferred that route. We were making enough money for their drugs and some food to feed the family. I knew it was wrong, and I would talk to my brother about it. When I was eighteen, I ran away. I've always regretted leaving my brother behind, but I couldn't survive trying to feed him too. I ended up cooking in a restaurant, making good enough money, and I stayed in a room above the kitchen. It was OK for a while, but then the owner started wanting sex too. I ended up running away to this commune, and I feel safe here. No one messes with me as long as I follow all the rules. It's so much better than anything else I've had in my life. Rachael, you must know that this is not a bad place to live. You must never try to run away again."

I reply, "I know … and I promise I'll be good. Why don't you try to find your brother one of these days? I'll help you find him. I'm a good investigator."

Cook replies, "Yep. I know that. It's why you're being punished so severely right now, right?"

I don't reply. I know she is right.

CHAPTER TWENTY-FOUR
BACK HOME INVESTIGATIONS

Gary is going out of his mind because there have been no leads. Mama and Dad are watching the kids every day while he is working with the police on Rachael's disappearance. Gary works at the school every day and goes to the police station at night. The whole family is so worried about Rachael. Where did she go?

Gary decides to come clean with Officer Dale. He knows that he has to tell the whole truth about Rachael. Maybe this will help the investigation. He calls and makes an appointment with Officer Dale.

As he walks into Officer Dale's office, he says, "I've got to tell you more information about where Rachael may be. When she went through the whole ordeal last year, she told me something that we did not share with you. I think I have to tell you everything."

Officer Dale takes out his notebook and says, "Go ahead, I'm going to write down everything. It's about time you started being honest with us."

Gary says, "When Rachael escaped from the commune last year, she told me she stabbed a man and a woman. Rachael had a marriage ceremony with Jerry, but she was not legally married to him. Well, Cindy was the friend who picked her up on the side of the road when Rachael tried to escape from Harold. She had caught Jerry and Cindy in bed together."

Officer Dale stares at Gary and says, "Go on."

"She said she flew into a rage and stabbed both of them. She took Cindy's car and escaped from the commune. She drove for a long time and stopped at a motel. After a shower, she put in the bloody knife and dress in a bag. She tried to get some rest and then drove to her parents' house. When she got there, she couldn't find the knife or dress anywhere. She was convinced that it was all a dream and that she never killed those two people. She begged me not to tell and said she would work with a psychologist and a therapist. She was convinced that she was not a murderer. She didn't want to go to jail. I don't believe she could kill anyone. She wouldn't hurt a fly, sir."

"Keep going." He Officer Dale is writing in his notebook as fast as he can.

Gary continues, "She is in that yellow car right now. She took it to her so-called sleep study. Rachael has been hiding the car behind our house and said she would return it soon. I think she went back to the commune to return it. I'm not sure if she went back or if she was kidnapped. She is an honest person and would not lie to me. They probably got her."

Officer Dale asks, "Didn't you say that your wife's therapist might know where the commune is? He used to have a patient who lived there. Maybe Rachael gave him some clues about where it is. If we find the commune, we will find Rachael." He calls the therapist and asks Spencer to come down to the station. He shakes his head. "Spencer should be here in thirty minutes."

Gary replies, "I'm so sorry we didn't tell you the whole truth."

"I know Rachael did not tell me everything. She has done this before. Remember how she used to sneak out and investigate at Harold's house? She was probably investigating again and got caught."

Spencer walks in and says, "What has she done now?"

Officer Dale says, "I believe she is trying to find out if she is a murderer. Did she tell you that she might have killed Jerry and Cindy."

Spencer replies, "No, she hated talking about the commune. She thought I knew more about it than I was saying. She didn't trust me."

Officer Dale gets out a map and says, "Spencer, can you identify where the commune is? Didn't you say that you had another patient from the commune? Did Rachael say anything about the whereabouts of the commune?"

Spencer replies, "Rachael said it was over two hours away and was near a river. I remember her saying it was hot there. I will look at my notes to try to identify what my patients said about the commune and let you know. Right now, I can't tell you where the commune is. I will check my files and get back to you."

Officer Dale says, "If we find this commune, we will find Rachael. Spencer, look at this map again and see if you see the river she was talking about."

Spencer takes a look and says, "Officer, let me look at my notes—and then I will get back to you."

Gary says, "There's no telling what they have done to her. Please hurry and find her for me. I don't think she killed anyone. Rachael would not—and could not—murder anyone. I'm going crazy. Please find her."

Officer Dale says, "I will do my best to find Rachael as soon as possible. I have all kinds of investigations in place. Spencer, get me that information by tomorrow morning. We cannot sit on this. Every hour counts."

CHAPTER TWENTY-FIVE
FEELING NOTHING

My mind and body are worn out from all the mental and physical torture. How much more can I take? I cry in bed, try to go to sleep, and think about my family. My memory is fading more and more each day. I can barely remember anything other than this commune. My mind is fuzzy all the time, and my thoughts are only about the fear of my dreams and what comes next at this awful place.

I wonder when they will trust me to get out of this terrible building. The House of Torture is a terrible place to be. I think I'm the first person who has been tortured in this building. If they don't kill me first, they will certainly have total control over my mind.

I'm falling asleep, and my last thoughts are about a guy named Spencer. Who is he? I should remember things like this, but after a few months in here, I'm confused about everything.

I'm lying on a couch, and Spencer is asking me about the commune. I think he is a bad guy, and he is trying to get too much information out of me. I see a clown picture on the wall. It falls off the wall, and glass is everywhere. Spencer picks up a piece and slices my arms in several places. I stared at my arms, but I feel no pain. The blood is dripping down my arms. I keep staring at them. Spencer starts yelling at me to tell him everything I know about the commune. He doesn't even see the blood. All he cares about is finding the commune. Who is this Spencer guy? I see the clown picture, and the clown jumps up and starts clawing at Spencer's face. I start running, and someone is chasing me. It is Leader Charles, and he is yelling, "Rachael, don't tell me where you are—or I'm going to kill you." I look back, and he has a knife in his hand and a cup of something that looks like Kool-Aid. He yells, "Rachael, you are not a Christian. You are a cult. You are so sick in the head, and I hate you." He lunges at me with his knife. I cry out as he cuts my throat.

I wake up from this dream feeling nothing. My dreams are so weird, and they don't make any sense at all. I'm amazed that I didn't start screaming when the clown was clawing Spencer's face. I think about Leader Charles and think he is a sick puppy. Is all the torture just conditioning me to take the pain and not say a word? I eventually drift back to sleep.

The wolves are chasing me in the woods again, and I'm running as fast as I can. I trip and fall. I'm crying and screaming as they are getting closer. Gary runs over and starts fighting them off with the iron rod that Leader Charles beat my feet with. The wolves start licking the blood on my feet. I start screaming, and then the wolves are eating something in the river. I can't see what it is until I run closer to the riverbank. Mice are floating everywhere, and Harold is standing in the middle of them. He is laughing at the wolves and doesn't appear to be scared at all. Spencer walks up beside me, and I tell him that everything is okay. I started quoting *Macbeth,* and Harold looks up at me and laughs. Spencer is also laughing at me. Both of these guys have evil written all over their faces.

I wake up crying in my bed. I remember how Gary tried to save me from the wolves. Oh, how scary Harold and Spencer were. Why do I have these evil dreams?

In the morning, Cook brings me breakfast. I don't even hear her. My dreams are so wicked. I wish I didn't have the night terrors.

Jerry walks in and stands over me with sexual hunger in his eyes. He removes my gown. I think he will be gentle because he loves me, but he ties my hands and feet to the bedpost. He rapes me repeatedly and says, "I will kill you if you run away again."

I am crying.

He slaps my face and tells me to quit crying.

My crying and screaming are making him more aroused.

He says, "I don't feel sorry for you, Rachael. You left me, and I thought you loved me. We even had a ceremony where you promised to live with me for the rest of our lives. What happened to your promise? Quit crying!"

"Jerry, please stop."

He replies, "I can't. You have to know that I love you, but I will continue to rape you until I feel that you are totally obedient to me, Leader Charles, and this whole damn commune. Do you hear me, Rachael?"

I reply softly, "I understand, Jerry."

Jerry rapes me again and is so worked up with rage. He is so rough and has no mercy on me. I cry inside because I didn't want to cry front of him. It makes him even angrier. Why do these guys get so sexually aroused when they are angry? I wish I could keep them from being mad at me.

As he walks out the door, he turns around and says, "Rachael, you are mine. Do you hear me? You are mine! This commune is a good place to live, but it can be a bad place too. Don't cross us again!"

I am in so much pain. I am bleeding, and every little movement hurts, especially between my legs. He put a cross inside me, and it tore my flesh. I am so sore and in so much pain. I am still mending from Leader Charles's beatings, and this rough sex is killing me. How much more can a person take? In my mind, I feel nothing, but my body is a different story. The pain overtakes me as I drift off to sleep.

My sisters and I are playing on floats on the river. I can't remember their names, but I know they are my sisters. I can see Joe, my brother, with a lot of friends, and they are swinging over the water with a rope. Dad is making sure it is safe. I look down at the river, and Harold is swimming in the shallow part. He is splashing and hitting something in the water. It looks like a floating body. I see blood in the murky water. Who has he killed now? I see blood on my hands. I see the murders at the river again. The water is murky. At first, I can't see what is in it. I then see blood mixed into the water, and people floating in the river. Red smoke is dissolving into the water, and the blood is floating over me. To my amazement, an inner tube floats beside me with a baby in it. The baby is sucking on a bottle and appears to be fine. Veronica runs over to me and tells me to run. I start running so hard. I hear someone behind me. I continued running, not knowing who it is, and I scream.

I wake up screaming and am so frightened in the dark. The covers have fallen off the bed, and I am so cold. As I reach down to get them, I feel pain in my body. Will I ever get out of this torture house? Will it ever stop? Will I ever be rescued? I have so many questions that I don't know the answers to. I know there are people from my past who love me. I can't remember who they are, but I wish they would come to save me.

CHAPTER TWENTY-SIX

PROBATION TIME

I think I've been in this house for about two months, but it may have been longer. Will I ever see daylight again? I don't even know who I am—much less anyone else I've known. My mind is foggy most of the time. In the back of my mind, I remember there have been good people in my life who have not tortured me like this. I have some good days, and I try to concentrate on the past. A few memories come back to me, but they are very seldom. Who are these good people I knew in the past? I'm starting to only remember this commune, and there is no past.

The movies and the asphyxiation continue on a daily basis. For the past week, the rapes and beatings have stopped.

Leader Charles and Jerry walk into my building, and I wonder what is going to happen to me today.

Leader Charles says, "Rachael, today we are going to let you walk outside for a short while. We need you to get stronger. If you try to run away, the torture will begin again."

"Yes, sir."

Jerry says, "You will only walk from this building to the garden and then back. You will be always watched by people in our flock. Do not disappoint us."

Leader Charles says, "Cindy has packed this bag of clothes for you. Please put on something presentable. We will be back in fifteen minutes. Be ready."

All I need to do is brush my teeth, put on some clothes, and comb my hair. The last thing I will do is put on the comfortable shoes that Cindy packed for me. My feet are still sore from the beatings. I will probably walk funny since they still hurt. I will be ready in less than fifteen minutes. My brain is going wild with thoughts of freedom. I am going outside. I am excited and scared. Will everyone be staring at me?

Jerry takes me outside, and my eyes slowly adjust to the sunlight. It is so bright and so beautiful in the commune. I wonder why I ever wanted to leave. Our commune is such a happy place, and the followers are always smiling and laughing. They just love it here, and I'm sure I will love it too. I continue walking with Jerry beside me, but every footstep hurts. My feet are swollen, and I think I have an infection.

Jerry says, "What is wrong with your feet? Why are they swollen and red?"

I refrain from telling him what Leader Charles did to my feet. I don't want the two of them getting into a fight. I guess Leader Charles decided not to tell Jerry about it. "Jerry, it's OK. My feet are not used to these shoes. They will be fine in a few days. I will get used to them."

He says, "OK, but if they get worse, please tell me. I will have to take you to the medical person. You may need some medicine."

"OK, I will." I wonder why Jerry is being so nice. He is mean to me most of the time. I will never tell him about the metal rod that

Leader Charles used on my feet. He might use it on me again if he finds out I have spoken about the punishment.

Cook is working in the garden with some of the other followers. No one looks up from their work. I know they have been told to ignore me and not give me any attention. They are growing corn, okra, beans, tomatoes, peppers, and squash. I wonder if they grow their own potatoes. It is the best garden I've ever seen. I look toward the back and see watermelons and cantaloupes. Seeing all this healthy food being grown lifts my spirits. It can't be that bad here, can it?

Jerry walks me back to my building. I wish they would let me stay out longer. It's so beautiful here, and everything is so green. I can't wait until I can start talking to everyone. My mind is so twisted from the brainwashing, but this commune is such a happy place.

Jerry tells me to get back on the table, and he straps down my arms and feet. I'm so disappointed that I have to endure this again. I thought it was over. Will it ever stop? He turns on the wild movie, and I feel so confused as my dreams continue.

I'm chasing Harold down to the river. I trip and fall and land on something. As I look to see what it is, I see a large rat underneath me. I scream and jump up and start running again. Harold has already made it to the river. He has two knives with him, and he looks at me with a blank stare and hands one of them to me. I want to stab him, but I am too scared. Instead, I take the knife and throw it into the river. Harold gets mad at me, and he throws his knife at me. It doesn't cut me at all. He jumps into the river and starts swimming. He is looking for the knife I threw. He finds it and jump out of the water and runs toward me. I stand there frozen as he grabs me. I look over and see Harold, and his eyes are glowing red. He has my knife in his hand. He starts coming toward me, but then he turns away. Joe runs up to Harold and starts talking about a mouse. Joe is wearing a swimsuit. I think, *That is odd. It is dark outside.* I am staring at the them as they are playing with a mouse. Joe walks away and goes toward the river to swim. Harold grabs me in the dark, and I scream.

After a few hours, Leader Charles comes and gets me off the table. He doesn't talk to me, and I don't talk to him. I'm sure he wants to have sex with me again. He has been abusing me every night.

He makes me sit up, and he removes my gown. At least he doesn't rip it off. He ties up my hands and feet. I guess he loves bondage sex. As he is raping me, I think about that man named Spencer. It helps to focus on other things and not on the rape. I try to remember anything from in my past, but I can only remember the commune. Spencer is the only person who keeps popping into my brain. I know he has to be someone important because I remember him. He looked like a nerd, and he talked about this commune all the time. What is up with that? Who is Spencer?

Jerry comes into my building, and I wonder if he is after happy seconds. Maybe he doesn't know what Leader Charles is doing to me. Jerry has sexual hunger in his eyes, and he crawls into the bed with me. To my surprise, he just holds me. Does he feel sorry for me?

"Jerry, I'm glad I'm back here with you. We had a good relationship when I was here last time. I'm so sorry for running away."

He says, "Rachael, don't leave me again."

"I won't … I promise you."

CHAPTER TWENTY-SEVEN
HAPPY FREEDOM

Cook enters my building this morning with a smile on her face. She informs me that she is taking me to the canteen for breakfast. I wonder why she was sent since she was probably needed in the kitchen. Why are they giving me freedom? I know it's just a test to make sure I won't run away again. Small steps.

"Rachael, get dressed. You're going for breakfast with me at the canteen."

"Really? What fun this will be! I will get to see all the happy people again."

Cook sits down while I get ready. My feet are doing much better. I hope Leader Charles never hits my feet again. I can't wait to see all my friends. I hope they remember me. All I remember is that this is a very happy place, and I'm proud to be here. I'm ready, and Cook opens the door. The sunlight hurts my eyes.

As we are walking toward the canteen, she says, "Rachael, don't be alarmed if the followers don't talk to you. They are leery of you since you ran away. You are just an outsider to them. Just like with Leader Charles and Jerry, you will have to gain their trust again."

I reply, "I won't be offended. I will just be friendly and smile."

Cook says, "If you are good, you may get to work with me again. I'm not sure how soon. You still need to work on things in your life and in your mind. Never bring up anything from your past."

I whisper, "I won't. You'll never know what I've been through in the past few months. I will never talk about it to anyone."

"That's the best thing for you. You don't want to get in any more trouble, right?"

"Yes, ma'am."

As I enter the canteen, Leader Charles and Jerry look at me intently. They want to make sure I act right and don't cause any problems. I will not do anything that is against any of the rules here. I will be as good as gold. I can't forget they both have done some terrible things to me here, but I'll still be good.

Cindy says, "Rachael, you can sit at my table if you want to."

"I can't, I must eat with Cook today."

"OK, whatever." She walks away.

"I'm sorry, Cindy. I'm still in trouble."

After breakfast, Jerry walks me back to my building. He tells me that I must get on the table again. He ties me up and starts the movie about the happy commune. I know every line by heart. I love this movie. My life is getting back on track, and I know I will have so much fun here. I've got to maintain this way of thinking to survive here. I'm ready to start again at this commune and fit in with everyone. Eventually, they will all trust me again.

At dark, Leader Charles comes and gets me off the table. He tells me to clean up and put on my gown. I know what is going to happen to me, but I'm not even disturbed about it. I guess I'm getting used to this nightly ritual. Maybe, one day, he will not want me anymore. I'm surprised he doesn't tie me up. He just has rough sex with me and leaves. Maybe he trusts me enough now that he doesn't have to tie me up. I don't know why, but I think I'm gaining trust from this fearless leader.

In bed, I start thinking about Spencer again. He is the only person I can remember. I'm not sure who he is though. I dreamed about him, but I don't think it was real. Spencer was significant in my past life, but I can't remember who or what he is in my life. I try to remember anyone else from my life. My brother had his head cut off in one of my dreams. Was that even my brother. Do I have brothers and sisters? What about my parents? Who are they? As I drift off to sleep, my mind is foggy again. Have I been brainwashed that much? What have they done to me?

I'm sleeping in my bed, and Gary is in his boxers. His boxers have clowns all over them. I laugh at him, and he runs away from me. I start chasing him. He runs into a room, and two dogs are sleeping in a baby bed. The dogs wake up and start crying. All of a sudden, two babies are crying. I remember John and James. They are playing together and keep saying, "Mama." I see Ryan and Sarah. They are dressed up in clown suits and are running through the woods. Gary appears with a knife. He is chasing them, and then we all go swimming in the river. I see bodies everywhere, They are floating on top of the water. They all have red clown wigs and their eyes cut out. I see fire all over the top of the river, and it is burning everyone floating in the water. I look everywhere for Harold, but all I see is his father. He is running wildly toward me. I run as quickly as I can through the woods. He reaches out and grabs me as I scream.

I think it is important that I remembered something about a man named Gary and two babies. What a weird dream. Who are they? Spencer, Gary, James, and John were all in my past life. I've got to figure this out. I can't tell Leader Charles, Jerry, Cook, Cindy, or anyone else at this commune what I remember from my dreams. They must all believe that I am completely brainwashed. I must keep this secret.

I think about this dream for hours. My subconscious mind brought it back to my memory. Thank you, Lord, for giving me back some of my memory. My dreams have saved me, but I can't tell anyone. This has to be a secret as I work to find out more about my past life. I know there must be more to my life than this commune.

Why am I so worried about my past? I have a future here. I remember my favorite scripture from the Kings James Version of the Bible. I memorized it. It is Jeremiah 29:11: "For I know the thoughts that I think toward you, saith the Lord, thoughts of peace, and not of evil, to give you an expected end." I must believe and not forget anything from my past. I must not forget.

CHAPTER TWENTY-EIGHT
SECRET MEMORIES

Leader Charles and Jerry enter my building for my daily asphyxiation ritual. I have grown accustomed to being strangled and then fainting when my oxygen has been cut off. I actually feel high right before I lose consciousness. I will never let them know this torture makes me feel good. I'm getting used to watching the movies after they nearly kill me. I really don't mind it.

After they leave, Cook brings me breakfast. I wonder what she thinks about me. She is very chipper and tells me that she has been informed that I can come out of the house at least twice a week. I think it will help me regain my strength. I need to see all the followers at the commune and make friends with them again. This commune is my happy place, and I'm excited to be here. The movies have taught me so much about this place. The followers are genuinely happy to be living here. I will be happy here too. This is such a fun place to be.

After breakfast, Leader Charles enters my building. I think he is going to strap me to the table again. Instead, he grabs my arm and walks me to my bed. He straps my arms and legs to the posts. Oh no, what is he going to do to me today? He removes the choking strap from his pants as he undresses. He rips off my gown and starts choking me with the strap as he has rough sex with me. I can't believe he is suffocating me during this. I feel increased sexual arousal and have an orgasm. When Leader Charles sees this, he stops and starts slapping my face. He does not want me to enjoy anything during his rapes. He wants all the pleasure. Did this really happen to me? I bet he won't choke me again while he is raping me. He did not get the pleasure he was seeking.

He dresses himself, picks me up, and places me on the table. He straps down my wrists and ankles. He turns on the weird movie and walks out the door. I feel humiliated, and I start crying. My situation is very bad. When will it ever stop? I eventually drift off to sleep.

Gary has entered my building, and he has a choke strap in his hands. I can't believe that Gary, the love of my life, is going to use that on me. Gary is my husband, and I live in a small town. Gary walks over to the table, and he stares at me. Leader Charles comes in and tells Gary to leave and never come back. He tells Gary that I don't remember him. I am on the table with tears rolling down my face. My mind is so foggy, and I can't remember anyone. Gary walks out the door. Suddenly, I'm free. I am running from the different buildings, and then wolves are chasing me. They catch me, and then blood is everywhere. They chew on my face and hands. I am screaming, I am so scared. I am bleeding everywhere. Then, all of a sudden, Jerry and Leader Charles are raping me. They tear off my dress. The wolves are watching. They do not come near Jerry or Leader Charles. I guess they are scared of these two very scary men. They are so evil. The wolves just wait, and then they jump on top of me and start biting and tearing my flesh. It hurts so badly.

When I wake up with a scream, I remember my dream. I remember my husband, Gary. The commune may be brainwashing me, but, in my dreams, I remember my family. I love them so much. I know they love me too. I hope they rescue me soon.

I then focus my attention back on the movie. What is the purpose of the weird sounds and shapes? I guess it makes my brain go foggy, and then I can't remember anything. I hate this movie, but I have to watch it. There's nothing else to do.

I need to be careful about my past. My sweet memories of my loved ones are still there, but they are only in my dreams.

CHAPTER TWENTY-NINE

WALKS WITH CINDY

Leader Charles and Jerry have slowed down their torture on me. I don't know why. I am allowed to go to the canteen with Cook twice a week. I'm also allowed to walk around the commune. I have to be supervised, but it is mostly with Cindy. I like Cindy so much, and all the followers have been fabulous. They are friendly again and ask if I'm doing better.

Cindy says, "I was hoping you wouldn't be mad at me for sleeping with Jerry."

"Yes, at the time, I was so angry at both of you that I could have killed you. It's a good thing I'm not a murderer, right?"

She says, "Yep, I guess we're lucky about that. Anyway, I don't like Jerry at all. I was just trying to get back at Bill for something. Let's talk about my old boyfriend, Bill. He left here right after you did. Did you hook up with him?"

"Heck no. I didn't have anything to do with him. Bill was weird and had all those special needs. He was high maintenance, and I wanted nothing to do with him. I was so worried that he hit you when he didn't get his way. Anyway, let's change the subject."

Cindy laughs and says, "I understand things were not so good at the time. I'm just glad he left. It will be better for you this time. Just wait and see. This is a great place to be!"

"Yes, I love it here so much. This is a great commune, and the followers are so happy and friendly. We're all just hippies, living the good life. Commune living is the best, and I never want to leave."

As we are walking by the laundry house, I see Bettye and wave. She looks so happy and peaceful. I'm in my happy place, and I will never run away again.

Cindy says, "You won't believe this, but Bettye has a new boyfriend. He is new, and they hooked up immediately. I'm so happy for her. By the way, I have a new boyfriend too. His name is Frank, and he has muscles like you wouldn't believe. He is so nice, and he never gripes at me. Have you seen him with me when you get out?"

"Yes, I saw him. It's nice that you met someone good. You needed someone who doesn't gripe all the time about meeting his needs."

She laughs and says, "I've got to go. I have to do my chores. I'm working in the kitchen with Cook. I'll see what I can do to get you in there next. It will be fun, and we will have a blast. Cook is playing music for us."

I hug her and say, "That would be nice."

Cindy returns me to my building and tells me to rest and get well so I can start doing chores soon. I'm very tired, I drift off to sleep immediately.

I'm running through a wooded forest with my sneakers on. I see a large tree, and I sit down beside it.

Detective Dale walks up to me without making a sound. When he sits down beside me, I jump. I didn't hear him coming. I take my binoculars out of my pocket and realize that there is something else in there. It is a gold ring. I think it is my wedding ring. Where did it come from?

Detective Dale stares at it, but he says nothing.

I jump up and run away from him. Something is chasing me, and I jump into a car. A homeless woman approaches my car. I roll down my window to see what she wants. All she wants is one quarter so she can put it with the three quarters that she has so she can buy some gas for her car. As I give it to her, I look into her eyes—and I know I have to kill her. As my knife enters her heart, I kept staring into her empty eyes. I know I need to cut out her eyes so she looks like a Raggedy Ann doll with the crossed button eyes. I feel at peace when I take out a knife and cut out her eyes. I feel like she can't see me now. Blood is everywhere. It is all over my clothes. What have I done? I stop breathing.

I wake up and try to scream, but Jerry is on top of me. The choke strap is tied around my neck, and he is tightening it. Is he trying to kill me? I didn't even hear him come into my building. Was I sleeping that deeply in my terrifying dreams?

He yells, "Rachael, stop screaming. You will never leave me again. If you do, it's out of my hands. You will be killed by Leader Charles. He has done it before, and he will do it again. No matter what I say, it will be out of my hands."

"I know, Jerry!"

Jerry says, "I just remembered that Leader Charles told me you got off while being choked during sex. I will never do that to you again after this time. I want to watch you have sexual pleasure one more time."

He tightens the strap around my neck, and I lose consciousness.

I wake up on the cold table again. He has strapped down my wrists and ankles again. He turns on the commune movies and walks out of the room. He is so mad at me.

Jerry is jealous of Leader Charles and his involvement with me. I need to remember that Jerry loves me, and I have created friction between them. I need to think of more things that will make them mad at each other. Maybe Jerry will help me. He probably won't help me escape, but maybe he will keep the torture from being too bad for me.

Maybe this is the start of getting out of here. I can turn the two leaders against each other. Leader Charles is the leader, and Jerry is second-in-command. If they are fighting, maybe someone can rescue me. Who will rescue me? Wait, I love it here, right? I drift off to sleep.

I'm walking down the path where I hid Cindy's car. The path ends at the river. Harold is hitting something in the water. He is stabbing Ryan and Sarah. They look like puppets as they splash in the water. Cindy walks over and asks me where her car is. I point toward the large bush. She slaps my face and starts walking toward her car. Harold runs over to me with the bloody knife. I start running through the woods, and Harold is chasing me. I turn around and take a nail gun and shoot him several times. It is so weird in my dream. I feel no emotion about hurting him. He is a killer. It is either him or me. I realize that Harold's spirit is chasing me. It is a ghostly figure. I see a red rooster coming after me, and I grab its neck and wring it until there is blood everywhere. It is either him or me. Someone is still coming for me, and I run.

I wake up shaking, but I don't scream. I guess I'm getting used to the night terrors. I drift off to sleep again as the dreams continue.

I'm walking beside the bleachers at a baseball game, and Harold is staring at me. I watch him as he slips into the dark. I see a girl with him. I wonder if he has a girlfriend. He has a knife and cuts the girl's throat. No blood comes out at all. Veronica walks up to the girl and starts talking to her. I think I'm seeing things. Harold walks away from the field, but then he turns back and says; "You're next." He slowly walks away into the dark. It is so dark, and I can barely see through the blood in my eyes. My next victim is my Valentine's Day date from when I was sixteen years old. He seems so sweet, but when we get in his car to go home, he wants to touch me in hidden places. He is nothing like Gary, but he is exciting at the same time. After a while, I am actually enjoying his touches. I climax, and I decide it is time to kill him. I think killing arouses me immensely, and I want more. I take a dagger out of my purse and pierced his eyes in crosses. He can't see that my sexual feelings bother me and embarrass me.

I wake up and remember the dream. I'm very scared about what my future holds.

CHAPTER THIRTY
SCARY MOVIES

Cook arrives at my building, and I'm still asleep. She startles me, and I jump up from my bed. My night terrors have been keeping me awake. I'm just so tired. I try to smile at her as I sit up.

She says, "It's time to get up, girl. You're going to the canteen today!"

I reply sleepily, "Oh, OK. It will just take me a minute to get dressed."

"I'll wait. You know, girl, you got to do right around here, and you won't get in trouble. This commune has been good for me, and I love it here."

As we are walking to the canteen, Cook is acting nervous. She is wringing her hands and looking from side to side.

I ask, "Cook, what is it? Who do you see? Are you scared of something?"

She replies, "I'm fine, Rachael. Everything is OK. Don't ask questions. This is a great place to live. Don't start thinking bad things."

I say, "OK, I won't."

Cook was so chipper this morning. While she was in my building, she was fine. As soon as we went outside, she started acting different. What is wrong with her?

In the canteen, Cindy and Bettye are talking in the drinks area.

Cindy turns around and walks up to me. She is wearing a long bohemian skirt and a bright purple shirt. She looks so cute, and her hair is in a bun. She seems so free.

Cindy says, "Did you hear what happened last night? We had strangers in our camp last night. They said it was a motorcycle gang. We have been told they meant no harm, but everyone is nervous this morning."

I reply, "I know. Cook was looking around everywhere when she was walking me over here. She was scared and jittery. Why does everyone freak out when anyone comes here?"

What are they hiding here? After we get our food, we sit down with other followers. They are so happy it is Wednesday, and we will be having church service tonight. I hope they let me go. There is a daily Bible study that they call "Morning Celebration." Wednesday nights are called "Worship Night," and there is singing and shouting and a sermon by Leader Charles. On the other nights, they had a service called "Night Life." I really want to go to all these church events, but so far, I have been stuck in the torture house. When will they let me out?

The followers continued talking about all the things they were learning about the Lord and how happy they were to be at the commune. I totally agree with them. I love it here. Everyone is so happy. Communes are the best life that could be given to a person. All the followers feel safe here until someone from the outside arrives.

We continue eating and talking, and it is so good to be out of my hellhole.

I whisper, "Cindy, can you ask Jerry if I can go to one of the services today?"

She says, "Yes, I will, but you need to understand that you are not trusted here. I know you want to worship with us, but you broke that trust when you ran away. I will ask, but they might not let you attend."

I reply, "Maybe one day I will be trusted again and can attend everything there is here. I heard they even have yoga and meditation classes here. I believe I need both of them. Do you know if it is one class?"

Cindy replies, "Yes, you go to both of them at the same time. I believe it will help you. I will ask permission for you to attend them."

I reply, "Thank you so much, Cindy!"

Cindy walks me back to my building and goes to do her chores.

Leader Charles and Jerry walk into my door.

Leader Charles says, "Rachael, we will be doing something a bit different with you today. Everything we are doing is for your own good. Today, you will go back on the table, but you will be watching horror movies. We think we have found the scariest movies there are. You will not be able to stop watching them because you will be tied up again. You will be working on not having your night terrors. You have to fight fear with fear."

Jerry says, "You must not scream at all. We will be watching closely."

Leader Charles grabs me.

I kick and scream as he places me on the table.

Jerry holds me down, and they strap me down.

I stop fighting because I'm so weak. Jerry gets very close to my face and sneers at me like he hates me. I thought he said he loved me. Is he just putting on a show for Leader Charles?

I scream, "This is not going to help me. It's going to make my nightmares worse."

Leader Charles says, "Shut up, Rachael. This will help you. Fight fear with fear!"

Jerry turns on the scary movie, and they walk toward the door.

Leader Charles stops and turns around. "Rachael, I will kill you if everything you are going through doesn't work out for us. Don't forget it!"

I reply weakly, "I know, and even though this is awful, I believe in this commune. I will do good, and I will show you."

They turn out the lights, and the movie starts. I start screaming. I can't help myself. I keep watching *The Exorcist*. I have heard about it, but I have never watched it. A girl starts floating above her bed, and she is speaking in tongues. She has the evilest face I've ever seen. It is so scary, and I am shaking all over. A priest performs an exorcism to try to get the devil out of her. The girl's bed shakes, and her face is so white. When her head starts twisting around, I scream again.

However, no one comes in the front door. I thought Leader Charles and Jerry said someone would be watching me. Maybe someone is watching me, but I don't know.

CHAPTER THIRTY-ONE
SCARY THINGS IN THE DARK

I am watching scary movies on the torture table. Today, I'm being forced to watch a spider movie. There are spiders in this haunted house, and as people walk through it, the spiders attack them. They are biting these people all over. A man is in bed, and the spiders build a web all over him. I cannot even see the man. A large white spider web is covering the bed. It's the largest spider web I've ever seen. I'm so scared but I have to refrain from screaming. Someone is watching.

The next movie is about scary clowns. They have jagged teeth that are black and have blood dripping from them. They have sharp vampire teeth. I close my eyes as a clown grabs a girl and bites her neck. The girl is screaming, and I start screaming too. I can't help myself. Another girl is running from another clown. This clown has the most awful makeup and claws instead of fingernails. He scrapes the skin off the girl's arms.

The girls are screaming and running away. There are so many clowns, and they are torturing the girls. I feel sorry for them and know they are about to die. I am shaking all over and have goose bumps on my arms and my head. I close my eyes.

I can't watch any more of this horror, but the next movie starts. To my dismay, it is a video of a boy killing two children at a river. I'm confused. Didn't that happen at my river? I lived near a river a long time ago. He cuts their eyes out, runs away, and grabs a girl in the woods. She is wearing red sneakers. As he grabs her, she screams. Why did Harold have to kill Sarah and Ryan? They were my friends.

I come out of the bathroom and quietly enter our bedroom. Harold is lying on his side, and I am watching him. Why is Harold in my bed? I go to the end of the bed, and blood is seeping out from the floor. I look down at my hands, but there is no blood on them. I watch as a girl enters the bedroom and hits him over the head with a hammer. He never makes a sound. I guess the intruder has killed him. Mama walks into the room and tells me to hold her hand. I put my hand in hers and look at the bed again. No one is in the bed. It is empty. I climb into it and go to sleep, but I awake abruptly to the sound of a hammer coming down on my head.

I wake up, and I am shaking all over. I have dreamed about the childhood murders that happened in my past. I'm remembering my old life through my dreams. Why is my mind so warped? Why do these leaders at this commune think these scary movies are going to help with my dreams? All it does is put thoughts in my head. Don't they know this by now? The last time I was here, fear did not help me. It just made my dreams worse. I will be dreaming about spiders and clowns tonight. What are they thinking?

The next movie starts, and it has zombies In it. Where did they get all these scary movies? They are dressed like mummies and are walking around graveyards. I close my eyes as one of them grabs a man and slices his neck with a knife. The dead man falls to the ground. I start screaming, but I know someone is watching me. The zombie grabs more people and kills them with knives and their claws. As the movie continues, there are flies and maggots all over the dead people. I am sick to my stomach. I turn my head and close my eyes to keep from looking at the scariest thing in my life.

I watch three or four movies, and I wonder when someone will stop them. The fear is so intense that I can barely breathe. I've never seen scary movies like this before. I hope they don't make me watch them much longer.

Jerry walks into the building and flips on a light. I can hardly see him because the light hurts my eyes.

Jerry says, "Have you seen enough, Rachael? You've been watching these movies for quite a while. All day and night should be enough for right now. Leader Charles and I have done tremendous research, and from all accounts, this is the way to stop your bad dreams."

I reply, "Jerry, it's not helping me. Tonight, I will be dreaming about spiders, clowns, and zombies. Don't you realize that I dream about what is in my head. You are putting bad things in my brain. I'll never be able to stop the horrendous dreams. My nights are full of terror, and you are making it worse."

Jerry says, "That's not true, Rachael. You won't even be scared of the dark after all of this. You will see that none of it is real, and you will relax. At night, nothing will scare you. You have seen it all now. This has been proven to help people with their night terrors. We have done so much research on these techniques. You will be watching these same movies over and over until you aren't scared of anything."

"You're wrong Jerry!"

He yells, "We are not wrong—just wait and see! Your mind will become accustomed to scary things, and you won't even blink after a dream. The dreams will become nothing to you. Rachael, someone will be back to feed you and put you in bed. It won't be me. I have things that need to be done around here. We are running a commune with many people here. You're not the only one who needs attention."

I'm stuck watching scary movies, and, as Jerry said, I'm becoming accustomed to them. The techniques that they are using on me are really out there. Are the followers really happy here? I keep telling myself that this is a wonderful place to live. Watching the happy commune movies has gotten into my brain. I drift off to sleep. I'm so relaxed and am finally able to ignore the scary movies they are showing me. I've seen so many of them that I've finally become accustomed to them.

I'm watching a scary movie about Harold and his father, Johnny. Johnny is making Harold bring people to him to sexually abuse and torture. This man is sitting in a chair, and Johnny is pulling off his fingernails. The man is screaming as the blood drips from them. He injects the man's neck with a drug. The man drifts off to sleep. Johnny laughs and makes a horrible sound. It sounds like a wolf call. I have goose bumps on my arms. Harold grabs the man and stabs him in the stomach. He looks at me and smiles. "You're next."

I am in bed, and the bed is filling up with blood. I grab for Jerry, but he is not there. Instead, it is Harold's father, Johnny, and his eyes have been cut out. I grab my pillow and start floating toward the end of the bed. As I approach the end, my pillow turns into a large bluebird. I fly away on him. I think I am going to be saved, but the bird throws me off his back. I am back in the bed of blood. Johnny is staring at me—even though he has no eyes. He grabs me.

I wake up screaming. I can't help myself. I'm so scared of Harold, Johnny, and all these scary people in my head. I remember Harold and Johnny from my past. I know they are bad and I don't want to dream about them again. I know who Harold is now. I know he killed my friends.

CHAPTER THIRTY-TWO
THE INVESTIGATIONS CONTINUE

Spencer is working with Officer Dale on Rachael's case. It has been a month or so that she has been gone. They have a lead on where the commune may be. His old patient said it could be close to a west Texas town, someplace where it is very hot and has a river flowing through it. Officer Dale has bulletins posted for a missing woman in all the major cities in Texas. There has been no information reported by anyone about where she could be.

Gary takes the boys to Mama and Dad every day. He goes to work at the school and talks to Spencer or goes to the police department to see if they have any new information. Gary is going out of his mind with worry.

As he drops the boys off, Mama says, "Gary, they will find Rachael, and this will all be over soon. I'm so nervous and scared for my daughter. Her life hasn't been so good with the terrifying dreams, her friends being murdered, and the problems with the commune. She is very resourceful, and I'm sure she will find a way to get out of this. Officer Dale is doing everything he can to find her. Spencer is helping too."

Gary replies, "I know. I have been praying for her all the time. I'm really freaking out. God is always there for us, and he has never forsaken us. I believe he will be here for her during this time, and she will be saved."

Dad says, "Our church has been praying for her too. Heck, the whole town is praying for her. I hope she is found soon."

Mama starts crying, "Oh my, I'm so scared. I know the police are working on this night and day. Her boys miss her so much. I don't mind watching them. They need us, and we are family. I hope they find her soon."

Gary says, "I hope so too. I love her so much, and I can't live without her. I've got her back. She can't be taken from me again. I hope no has murdered her. I need to quit thinking about this, but it's in the back of my mind all the time. I hope they don't find her in a ditch."

Dad pats him on the back. "She'll be back, son. We just need to keep our faith and know that God is with us and with her too. I have to believe that. Otherwise, I would go out of my mind. I miss my little girl so much."

Later that night, Officer Dale calls Gary and says, "We may have a lead. We think she is someplace close to Laredo, Texas. If she is there, we will find her. Come down to the station, and I'll catch you up on everything."

Gary hurriedly leaves. He is so excited that Rachael may be found soon.

CHAPTER THIRTY-THREE

THE WAY TO A BETTER LIFE

I can't believe my eyes as Cindy walks in with a tray of food for me. It looks delicious. I'm so hungry, but I'm also excited to see my friend. She turns off the movies and unstraps me from the table. As she is helping me sit up, she says, "Rachael, you know you had this all coming to you because you ran away. I would never run away. This place saved my life. Once you come here, you need to stay. They let Bill go away because he was not good for the commune, and he was not good enough for me. I'm glad he is gone."

I reply, "Thank you for helping me sit up. With your help, I believe I can walk over to the table. The food looks good, and I'm hungry."

"You will get out of here someday, and it will seem like a dream to you. Oh, I'm sorry. You have bad dreams all the time, right?"

"Yes. Cindy, I promise you and everyone else here that I will be good. I will not try to run away again. I want them to stop the torture and the horrible movies. I wish they would let me get out of this horrible building so I can go back to doing my chores. I want to go to all the religious services. I want to be a true part of this commune. I've watched the movies over and over about how communes are and how happy the people are. I truly want to be a part of that."

Cindy says, "Yeah right. Well, you screwed up before, girl! You will probably do it again."

"No, I won't … please believe me. I know I screwed up before, but I promise to do the best I can from now on. I love this commune. It is so happy here."

Cindy replies, "That's just the happy commune movies talking now, girl. You've watched so many of them that you don't know reality."

"I know they have tried brainwashing me. I know that. It's just that I know now that this is where I was always supposed to be in my life. Jerry loves me so much, and I made a covenant with him before all of you and God. I will not break my promise again. I feel a loyalty to this place now."

She says, "You better not break your promise—or you will be a dead girl."

Leader Charles opens the front door and says, "Cindy, get out of here. I need to talk to Rachael."

Cindy immediately gets up and leaves. Oh no, here come the rapes, the beatings, and the choking scenes. Leader Charles looks mad about something. I get up from the kitchen table and walk over to the torture table. I know what's coming.

He says, "No, go to your bed."

I sit on the bed.

He follows me and tells me to remove my gown.

Well, it won't be too bad. At least he didn't rip off my gown.

He takes off his belt and starts slapping my back. The belt is leaving marks on me. At some point, he draws blood. My back hurts so much, and then I go numb. I can't feel anything as he beats my back.

He screams, "Rachael, I know that you and Jerry have made eye contact. Do you think he will save you? I've talked to him, and he assured me that he's on my side. Don't go there—do you hear me?"

I reply, "Yes, sir."

He says, "Don't forget that I'm in charge around here. Jerry is my second-in-command, but I'm the leader. Do you want me to beat Jerry?"

I reply, "No, please don't beat Jerry. He is a good man, and I love him."

Leader Charles stops the beating and says, "After you heal, I will let you walk around the commune and attend the services here. You haven't earned all the trust around here that I expect, but I know you understand the consequences if you try to do anything against the rules. Many people will be watching you."

I start crying again. "I understand … thank you."

"I'm watching you all the time. You have crossed us before, but it will never happen again. I know you are trouble around here, but since you have made your way back to us, we will have to deal with it. Don't cross us again. It will be your life next time."

He leaves, and I'm grateful that he didn't rape me. I'm also grateful that I will get to go outside soon. My back is stinging, and I'm in excruciating pain again. I look at my bloody sheets. My back must look like hamburger meat. It is bleeding so badly. Leader Charles is a monster. I wonder how his childhood was. Was he beaten like this?

As I whimper on my bed, a guy in a white jacket enters my building. He looks like a doctor. He walks over to my bed and tells me to roll over. He washes my back with a soft towel and puts a salve all over my back. He doesn't talk to me at all, and then he leaves my building. My back feels better, but it still feels like raw meat. I don't dare move. Every movement is killing me. My back is on fire. Damn, the punishments around here are bad.

I remember that I have to follow all the rules and not run away. They have truly taught me that. Other than my dreams, I can't remember my past life. I only get bits of pieces of it in my night terrors. I drift off to sleep.

Harold is chasing someone toward the river. I'm hiding behind a tree and watching with my binoculars. I hear laughter and splashing down by the swimming area. All my friends are floating on their inner tubes. Everyone looks so happy.

Harold throws a cat into the shallow end of the river. There are large rocks everywhere.

I stay behind the tree.

Harold turns and stares at me. He knows where I'm hiding, and he smiles at me.

I am floating on an inner tube, at the new river, with Jerry. He is holding my hand. I look over, and Leader Charles is watching us from the riverbank. I see another couple, Frank and Sherry, and they are swimming toward us. As they get close, I notice that they have no clothes on. Jerry doesn't seem to notice and starts talking and laughing with them. I glance over at Leader Charles, and he has a frown on his face. I then see Frank and Sherry in the rapids. They are going down the river fast. Neither Leader Charles nor Jerry tries to help them.

As I wake up, I'm not screaming or crying. This is just another dream that is putting together all the pieces of my past life. I start praying to God for his healing. I need a miracle. I need to get myself out of this predicament. Why do I always find myself in difficult situations? I guess I need to get closer to God and stop all my shenanigans. I'm not invincible. They are going to kill me here. The only thing I can remember at this point is what I dream about. Since my dreams are so extremely horrendous, they are not something that I want to remember.

Will my dreams ever go away? I drift off into my dreams again.

A knife is in my hand, and blood is all over on my bed. Someone is trying to get in the back door. I can hear them using a screwdriver on the door. The door opens, but I can't see anyone entering. It is just a black hole with nothing standing on the other side. Dad walks outside with his flashlight and looking for anyone out there. He sees nothing unusual. He doesn't see anybody. All I can see is darkness and the light coming from his flashlight. Dad goes back to bed. As I get back in my bed, I notice the knife in my hand and the blood.

A spider is in the bed with me. I feel it crawling up my arm. I know it is a brown recluse spider. I jump up and grab a flashlight and try to find it. I can't find the spider anywhere. I go back to bed, and Veronica walks inside. She is wearing pajamas with spiders all over them. She laughs and says she is not scared of anything. She comes over and stares at me. I can't see anything but spiders.

As I awake, I am shaking all over. I really don't like spiders. What's up with me always having a bloody knife?

CHAPTER THIRTY-FOUR
A NEW DAY

After a few days of healing—with no torture involved—I start to get my strength back. I guess the bad guys know they have nearly killed me with the beatings. My front door opens slowly, and I wonder if it will be more torture or someone nice coming to see me. It's Cook, and she has come to take me to the canteen for breakfast.

She says, "Good morning, Rachael. Today is going to be a new day!"

Even though my back still hurts, I jump out of bed. I'm so excited about going outside. I'm proud to get to see everyone. I hope everyone still likes me. I know it will work out this time. I love all these people here. This is a good place to live. I believe this in my heart. When I go to church, I will be jumping for joy and thanking my Lord for saving me. I guess I'm truly brainwashed now.

We walk to the canteen, and many followers start clapping and getting up to greet me. I wonder why they are making such a big deal about me being back. One the followers tells me that I'm just like the prodigal son who has come home. They are welcoming me back with open arms. I'm so happy, and even though my back hurts, I hug them as they come to me.

Leader Charles and Jerry come over to my table and smile at me, but I can feel the difference in their smiles. I'm not sure if they are being genuine or are trying to look good in front of everyone.

Leader Charles says, "Rachael, I expect you at Morning Celebration today. It starts soon. Eat quickly."

Jerry replies, "Welcome back."

As I am eating as fast as I can, Cindy walks over and sits down at my table. She hugs me and just sits there. I wonder why Ms. Chatterbox is not talking. Is she leery of me after all I have done? I finish eating, and we walk to the chapel. I can't wait to get there to thank God for being in a better place.

As I enter the chapel, peace comes over me. The music starts, and everyone is clapping and singing. I join in with them. Clapping my hands makes my back hurt, but I ignore it and take the pain. I'm used to going to church, but this service is a little different. It's more charismatic than I'm used to. The people are so joyous and happy to be living in this commune. It's all they have, and it's better than their old lives.

I used to go to church. I can't remember the name of the church or where it was. I think it must be near a river since I dreamed about one recently.

Jerry sits down beside me. Leader Charles may not want him near me. Jerry smiles at me and starts singing along with everyone. I join in again, truly praising God. He has been so good to me. Now that they have let me out, I'm in a good spot in my life. I have a wonderful place to live and so many wonderful friends.

Maybe Leader Charles will let me start my chores tomorrow. I feel like I am strong enough for cooking, working in the garden, or doing the laundry. I'm up for anything here at this commune, and I am ready to start my new life—without any torture.

Leader Charles goes up to the podium and says, "Good morning, my followers. Today, we have a prodigal child who has come home. She is right here in our service. She went astray for a while, but—thankfully—she returned to her flock. God always brings home the wayward. He leads them back to where they belong. I will read Luke 15:11–32 from the King James Version. Please rise as I read."

It is a long passage, but the gist of the story is that the father accepts his son back home after the son goes looking for a better life.

"We all know that this is the best place for each of you. I see and watch every day that you are happy. No one is mistreated here unless you disobey the rules. Our rules are not hard: just love God and each other. The Bible says to love one another, and I believe we will truly remain strong here if we do just that.

Everyone in the audience says, "Amen."

As the invitation starts, Jerry leads me down to the front.

The followers come forward, lay hands on me, and chant, "Heal her, Father. Heal her, Father. Heal her, Father."

As we are leaving church, Jerry grabs my hand. I let him do this because I don't want anyone to see me doing anything wrong. What is he thinking? Does he think we will start up just as we left things when I ran away? Jerry is not consistent in his feelings or the way he treats me. I am very confused by his actions. Some are bad, and some are good. I hate the evil that lives in him. I never know when it will come out.

Jerry says, "Rachael, I love you, sweetheart. I want you to love me again. I know we have been tough on you, but it had to happen. Everything happens for a reason."

"I know, Jerry. It's just been very tough on me. I hope things get better for me and our relationship."

As we walk up to my door, Jerry kisses my cheek. It is so sweet of him. I walk inside and get ready for bed. Things are going to be all right. I'm doing better and regaining their trust. I hope I have no more lessons to learn here. These types of lessons will kill you.

As I drift off to sleep, I hope I don't have any bad dreams tonight. I'm so tired, and I need rest. I need to let my back heal so that I will be 100 percent and able to work again.

I'm in bed, and a hand grabs me from behind. I start screaming and fighting it. Oh no! It's a clown—and he has a knife. The clown starts slashing my back, and I feel every cut. Then, for no reason at all, he stops and runs out my door. I wonder why there is no pain. Didn't he just cut my back? As I reach back, the bloody clown jumps on top of me and starts choking me. I scream. Leader Charles and Jerry are hitting me so hard. I start running into the woods, far away from them, but they capture me again and start beating me. I look, and the whip is covered in blood. When they catch me again, they turn me over and take turns raping me. I notice a knife in my hand. I turn over and stab Jerry in the leg. Leader Charles starts slapping my face. I see Harold and his father running toward us. Harold gets to me first and pushes Leader Charles off me. I see the knife in Jerry's hand, and he stabs Harold. I jump up and run away.

I wake up screaming. I am so glad it was a dream and not real. I thought the screams had left me. Why don't I have my sister here to protect me? Wait a minute … I remembered that I have a sister? Maybe I can remember more.

CHAPTER THIRTY-FIVE
CHORES BEGIN

As I awake, I worry that I won't get to go outside today. I remember my bad dream and worry that the torture will start again.

Cindy opens the door and says, "Hey, girl. Let's go to breakfast!"

I put on my sneakers. "I'm ready. I was so afraid I wouldn't get to do anything today. Yesterday was too good to be true."

"You will be working with Bettye in the laundry room. It's hot in there, and it's hard work. Jerry told me that its more enclosed, and they can watch you better in there."

"I know that I'm not to be trusted. They are afraid that I will run, but I'm not going to do it. I'm going to be good and take the blessings from getting to live here."

As we walk toward the canteen, Cindy tells me about her new boyfriend. "Frank is not like Bill at all. He's a nice guy, and I think I want to marry him. He has very large muscles and is so strong. I believe I'm in love with him. After love comes marriage, right?"

"Yes, of course. Just be careful. You go from man to man like you are changing your panties. You have to get it right and make the right choice."

"Did you know that, in the eyes of the Lord, you are still married to Jerry?"

What about my past life? Was someone named Gary my true husband? He was in my dreams. Who is he? Is he someone I was in love with? I also dreamed about the two babies who called me "Mama." Am I a mother? I noticed some stretch marks on my stomach. I guess I've been pregnant before and gained some weight. Cindy told me that I'm married to Jerry. I love this commune. Everybody is so happy here. She is still chattering as we line up to get our breakfast. I can't wait for my coffee. Caffeine will be good for my frail body.

Cindy says, "Rachael, did you hear me? You are still married to Jerry. Are you going to move in with him when you get out of your jail building?"

"I don't know if he wants to live with me. I have such scary dreams, and I wake up screaming. I used to scare him so bad. I'm a freak. Can't you see that?"

She replies, "Well, I'm sure that is over. You don't still have those dreams, right?"

I say, "Unfortunately, my dreams are really bad. I am tortured by night terrors, and I'm not sure if I will ever get rid of them. I hope they don't shock my brain here. I don't think those scary movies are working."

Cindy laughs and says, "Girl, it's not that bad here. Haven't you survived so far? You are a survivor!"

"I guess so."

Leader Charles and Jerry walk into the canteen. I hope they will leave me alone today. Maybe they think I'm brainwashed enough. I'm not going to let them know that I have some memories from my dreams of my past life. I'm going to pretend that the only thing I can remember is their torture. I'm going to love it at this commune, and I will show them that I love it here.

Perhaps my dreams will save me. If only someone would come and rescue me.

CHAPTER THIRTY-SIX
CINDY AND FRANK

After breakfast, Cindy walks me over to the laundry building and leaves me there with Bettye. She is working in the garden this week, and she is glad because she gets to see Frank from time to time. Bettye doesn't seem so happy to see me. I work alongside her, remembering what I did in the past with the laundry, but she doesn't talk to me. As I am working, I stare out the window.

I notice Cindy and Frank hiding behind a small building. I think it is the pump house. Cindy is holding Frank's hand, and they are talking intensely. He kisses her occasionally, and their talking continues. I wonder what they are talking about. Maybe they are talking about their marriage plans. I hope they are honest with each other and talk about their past lives. They don't need to start out with any secrets.

Cindy told me about her past. That girl used to be wild. Cindy was involved with alcohol and drugs. She ended up here after she hit rock bottom. She got clean in the commune by going to group sessions. She found the willpower to stop. She made up her mind that she was sick of the drugs, and she was done. She still smokes marijuana. She puts it in our coffee. She said it makes us happy all day. Maybe she got off the bad stuff and considers weed not too bad. She told me it is a plant that is grown in God's green pastures. She needs to tell Frank all about her past life; otherwise, their relationship won't work. Frank needs to tell her the truth about his life too.

Around noon, Bettye tells me that we are going to have lunch in the canteen. "Don't try anything. If you try to run away, I will take you down to the ground. I'm a strong person, and I have no problem with hurting you. I'm responsible for you, and I don't want to get in trouble. Things are never good when you get in trouble here. I found out the hard way when I arrived here."

"I know. I've been through total hell here. Did you get tortured too?"

Bettye says, "Don't talk about this with me or anyone else. In fact, don't talk to me at all. You are bad trouble here, and I don't want to be affiliated with you. I don't want to be mean to you, but that's the way it has to be."

"I know you don't want to get in trouble, but you don't have to be unsociable. I love it here, and everyone is so happy. I will never run away again!"

She mumbles, "That's just the happy movies talking."

I guess she had to watch the weird movies too. I don't suppose she had to watch the scary movies because I never heard her say anything about bad dreams. Hopefully, she didn't have to endure the rapes and beatings like I did.

As we enter the canteen, I see Cindy and Frank in line for food. They are holding hands and talking. It's good that they are communicating so well. I hope their relationship makes it. They eat quickly and walk out the door together. I wonder what they are in a hurry about. Are they up to something? They better be good—or bad things will happen to them. I haven't forgot the torture, rapes, or beatings.

As I leave the canteen with Bettye, I see Cindy and Frank talking to Leader Charles. None of them notices us as we walk by.

Frank says, "I'm watching her as close as I can. Let me know if you need any help with her treatments."

Bettye and I keep walking toward the laundry building, and I don't hear what Leader Charles says to Frank.

Frank is probably a spy. He is helping Leader Charles and Jerry watch me. I walk over to the folding table and start folding clothes. I'm careful to put the marked clothes in the correct baskets. I don't want to get in trouble by messing up.

Bettye is humming and putting clothes in the washers.

We have so much to do in here every day. There are more than fifty followers who need clean clothes. It feels like we are washing clothes for a hundred people. Maybe there are more followers here than when I left.

At the end of the day, Bettye walks me back to my building. I see many followers walking home from their chores. They wave at me and Bettye as we pass them. The day is almost over, and we will have Worship Night after dinner. I'm so excited.

Out of the corner of my eye, I see Cindy and Frank enter her building. I wonder what they are going to do. Is she having sex with him already? She is still living in the "House of Boho." It was decorated so cutely with the hippie style of bold and colorful boho art everywhere. She had a lovely tapestry on her wall with the sun, moon, and stars on it. I loved her velvet couch and colorful rugs. I wonder if she has been able to add anything to her art. When she picks up the medical supplies, she probably gets to shop a little too. There's no telling what she has now.

If I get assigned to a building—maybe back with Jerry—I can make it as beautiful as Cindy's house. I want my place to be peaceful and relaxing. I hope it will prevent the horrible dreams. Living in a lovely place will do the trick, and I will be able to control my dreams. I know it's wishful thinking, but I have to stay positive. When I move back into the House of Peace, I want to decorate it with happy and stress-free appeal. I will look for soft, neutral-colored pillows and light-fragrance candles. It will smell like we have fresh flowers all the time. Maybe Cindy will help me find some pictures for the walls. Were there any pictures taken when Jerry and I got married? I need to surround myself with happy memories. I want to feel safe and relaxed in my new home.

Why were Cindy and Frank able to go into her house? Does he live there with her now? Are they planning something? I'm so suspicious of everyone. Knowing Cindy, they are probably having sex.

Before Bettye leaves, I say, "Do you know why Cindy and Frank are in her building right now?"

She replies, "I don't know much about what goes on in this commune. I try to keep my nose out of things. This is what gets you in trouble every time. You're just too nosy, and you're always trying to figure things out. Just ignore what you see—and you will stay out of trouble."

"I know, but I'm so curious about what they are doing. Chores are over, and we all need to be getting ready for dinner and worship. I wonder if Frank lives with Cindy. I might be brainwashed, but I know that living together before marriage is not right. It's living in sin."

Bettye says, "Stay out of it!"

CHAPTER THIRTY-SEVEN

WORSHIP NIGHT LIFE

Jerry arrives to take me to dinner. He tells me that I'm "doing good," and he hopes I don't screw up. If I do, they will have to start the torture again. I know he is just reminding me so that I never forget what they did to me. I'm not leaving this commune again. This is the best place for me. This commune is my happy place. My night terrors are getting better. I rarely scream out loud. Maybe my nightmares and the screaming will end. I'm so full of hope.

As we are having dinner, Jerry says, "Rachael, never forget that table with the straps. To make sure, from time to time, we will have to repeat the process. I don't want you to forget what will happen if you disobey any of our rules. With you having nightmares all the time, you will need punishment along the way. I hope you don't have any when Leader Charles or I are around you. The punishment will be severe, and it will be back to the scary movies again, do you hear me?"

"I will dream ... so I might as well get used to my punishment. Will I get to move into another building and just go back to the punishment house when I get in trouble? It's sad that I'm predicting that I can't stay out of trouble."

"Yes, you will be moving in with me soon."

"That's fine with me. I will sleep on your couch ... so you can get your rest. I can't promise that I won't dream, but I will try with all my might not to scream and wake you."

He says, "You can sleep on the couch after we have some time together. I'm so excited to go to church with you tonight. You need to worship and get yourself back in line with your faith. It will be such a good feeling."

"Yes, I know. Jerry, I want to redecorate our place. I want to make it very peaceful. I will work with Cindy to get new soothing pillows and art to decorate from our clothing building. I know they have things like that in there."

He replies, "Get Cindy to help you. I want you to try to relax and stop all of those dreams. Your dreams awake me also and scares me like someone is getting us. I don't like that."

I reply, "I know."

As we are walking into the chapel, Jerry grabs my hand. I feel so peaceful and am ready to bow down to God and seek forgiveness. As we are praising God in music, I feel so loved by these wonderful worshippers. Everyone is singing, smiling, and clapping. Every once in a while, I see them looking at me. I nod to them and smile, and they smile back at me.

Leader Charles walks up to the podium and asks us all to bow our heads. He prays for all sorts of things. Mostly, he prays for forgiveness of our sins. "In the name of the Father, the Son, the Holy Ghost, and me." Leader Charles thinks he is part of the Holy Trinity. In church, I was not taught that way. I try to remember where I went to church, but nothing comes to mind. I hate that so much of my memory is gone. Will the memories be erased forever?

When the service ends, most of the followers say hello to me. I'm so happy here, and this is such a wonderful place to live. I'm so glad that Cindy gave me something cute to wear. I feel so calm and restful tonight.

Jerry walks me to my building, and I think I'm going to get to go to bed.

Maybe Jerry will want to make love to me.

Jerry leads me to the table and picks me up.

I start crying. "Why, Jerry? Why?"

He straps my wrists and ankles to the table and says, "Rachael, you must never forget this punishment. We have to keep it fresh in your mind. I have no other choice but to do this to you."

"I know, but why at night? I want to go to my bed."

"We don't want you getting too comfortable here. Someone will remove you from this table in the morning. Good night to you. I'm sorry, Rachael, but these are my orders from Leader Charles. I don't want to get into trouble like you are in."

"Jerry, why do you have to do what Leader Charles says? Don't you have any say around here?"

"Rachael, I'm second-in-command. I'm not the boss, and I cannot make all the decisions around here. Leader Charles ultimately tells all of us what is going to happen around here."

"Please take me to my bed, Jerry. I will make love to you. It will be so good—I promise."

"I'm not in charge. Do you hear me?" He turns on the weird sounds and shapes and walks out the door.

I guess my brainwashing is not over. Why do these shapes make me forget who I am and who I know? Oh no, the scary movies are on too.

I open my eyes, and Jerry is standing over me. He rips off the dress I was wearing at the service. He beats my face with his fists and kicks my stomach. He rolls me over on the floor and keeps kicking me. I think he broke my tailbone. When it stops, I see my brother Joe standing over him. Jerry runs away.

A man is chasing me, and I slip and fall into the bloody river. My head hits a rock. I am drowning and sinking in the bloody water. I start floating down the river. There are kids everywhere, and I start playing with them. We are laughing and playing and having so much fun. Harold and Johnny are down by the rocks, and they are staring at me. What can I do? I start running.

I wake up slowly. The dream seemed so real. Did all of that happen to me? I remember that I have a brother named Joe. Wasn't it Veronica, my little sister, who has always been there for me? Maybe my brother also loves me and wants to protect me. This is wild. I have a brother and a sister on the outside. I know they love me. I'm so confused. Do I want to live in this community or at home?

CHAPTER THIRTY-EIGHT
THE NIGHTMARES CONTINUE

I drift in and out of sleep on the torture table. Will the crazy movies ever stop? The table is so cold and hard. I wonder how much more my body can take. They have done so many things to me here. I think about how I will never be the same again as I drift off to my torturous sleep.

I'm running through the woods, and wolves are chasing me. They have blood on their teeth. As they get closer, I trip and fall. The ground is so hard. The wolves start eating Sarah and Ryan's faces. There is so much blood, and their eyes have been cut out. Someone has sewn large buttons over their eyes. I see their eyeballs beside them. Harold is laughing and watching me. He spins his head all the way around like the girl in *The Exorcist* and stares at me.

All of a sudden, a dark person is chasing me toward the river. As they get closer, a familiar face appears. The face looks evil, and it has scars on it. Where did the scars come from? I see blood on his hands. Is it Harold? Is it Johnny? He has a knife, and he is stabbing something in the river. I can't see what he is stabbing. I turn around and run away from the river as fast as I can. He is chasing me, but who is it?

I wake up screaming.

Leader Charles walks into my building. He looks so mad. He places the choking strap around my neck and chokes me until I lose consciousness.

I wake up in my bed. He rips off my grown and rapes me. I feel the strap around my neck. As it is tightening, I stare into Leader Charles's face. There is so much evil here. I lose consciousness again.

After he is through with me, he carries me to the table. I'm strapped down again, and he starts a scary movie about a haunted commune on the outskirts of a town. Everyone is getting killed there.

Leader Charles says, "Rachael, get it together. Quit the dreaming and the screaming. Take control of yourself. Watch this movie. It is a new one. Maybe it will scare you about communes—the bad ones."

I am naked and afraid. I don't want him to attack me again. I must be good here. Will I ever get to go outside again? I thought I was doing so well. Will I ever be trusted here again? Will they feed me?

Frank is on top of me, and he has the strap. Instead of putting it around my neck, he puts it around his own neck. As he pulls it tighter, his face turns red. His eyes are bulging out, and he loses consciousness. He is so heavy, and I can't breathe. I wish he would wake up and get off me. He awakes, and Leader Charles hits him on the head. There is blood everywhere, and it is dripping on me. Harold is standing in the background, and he is laughing again.

I stab Leader Charles repeatedly—just like Harold stabbed Ryan and Sarah—and I cut out his eyes like a Raggedy Ann doll. I have a needle and thread in my hand, and I start sewing large buttons over his eyes. He is not dead yet, and he screams in pain. However, as he screams, he just lets me do it. I feel no remorse for him. I don't care. Hi is an evil man, and he deserves a painful death.

I wake up screaming again. This time, no one hears me. I try to calm myself down and figure out my dream. Is Frank a good guy? Is he trying to help me? Is he a mean man who will hurt me when he gets a chance? I'm so cold. I have no clothes on. Leader Charles left me on this horrible cold table. Why do they think this type of torture will help me with my dreaming? Will anyone save me? I drift off to sleep again and into my tortured mind.

I'm am on a cold slab, and there is blood all over my legs. I look down and see a metal instrument being inserted between my legs. Blood starts pouring out. Leader Charles and Jerry are both there, and they are laughing at me. I see a tiny baby on the table. It is drinking from a bottle and sleeping. I feel a knife cutting my stomach, and there is so much blood.

All of a sudden, snakes are everywhere. They are trying to bite me. I am screaming and jumping around as they slither around me. They start biting me. Finally, my dad comes to my rescue. He steps on one of the snake's heads and tears it off with one of his tools. Suddenly, all the snakes disappear.

I wake up in the morning. I am more stressed than ever. I think I have the most warped mind in the world. Tears run down my face as I remember my lifetime of dreaming awful things.

The door opens, and I feel so humiliated. I am so exposed. I'm naked and have bruises all over me. I'm shaking with fear.

Bettye says, "Rachael, I'm here to get you ready for your day in the laundry building."

I reply, "Thank you so much. I've had a rough night."

"You'll make it."

As we are walking to the laundry house, I try to keep up with her. I am so sore.

Bettye doesn't seem to notice that I'm having problems walking. "Today is your last day working with me. Tomorrow, you will be assigned to another area. I mean it, Rachael, don't mess up here. They will try to kill you with all the punishment."

"Bettye, how do you know about the punishment? Did they do it to you? Please tell me. I need to know if others have suffered like I have. What kind of place is this?"

"Rachael, don't forget that this is a happy place. This commune saved my life, and it will save your life too. Remember your movies."

Bettye goes back to putting the clothes in the dryer and quits talking to me. I try to bring up the movie to her, but she just puts her hand out. I know this means she is done talking to me. I assume she knows about the movies. They must have done the same thing to her. I fold the clothes and think about the movies. The weird, happy, and scary movies are in my head now. When will this all end?

I am so happy at this commune. I enjoy doing my chores, and I enjoy the followers too. I especially enjoy going to church. This place makes me feel wonderful. I laugh as I think the brainwashing is working.

As I'm leaving for the day, I say, "I will see you again—maybe when we are eating in the canteen. I, for sure, will rotate through here again. Thank you for all your help."

She replies, "OK. You can go now. You need to get ready for dinner."

Bettye is a weird person. What did they do to her?

After chores, dinner, and worship, Jerry walks me to my door. I am so tired. I crawl into bed and go to sleep. No one tortures me, rapes me, or beats me tonight. Luckily, I have no dreams and am able to get some much-needed rest.

CHAPTER THIRTY-NINE
WASHING WINDOWS

In the morning, Jerry enters my building. I am already dressed and ready for breakfast.

As we walk outside, Jerry says, "Today, you will be washing the outside windows of all the buildings on the commune. Frank will be helping you since he is taller and can reach the top windows."

This will be a long job, and it's so hot outside. Why are they asking me to do something that is so hard? I guess I've got to get strong after my ordeal. I will probably get to see all the buildings and find out all their names. I've been in the House of Torture for so long that I'm ready to go to another building. One of them is probably called the "House of Death," and that frightens me. I don't want to have to go there. They will probably kill me there. My imagination is off the charts.

I reply, "OK, Jerry. That's fine with me. I don't have any other choice, do I?"

"Nope," he replies.

After breakfast, Frank walks over to our table and says, "Rachael, are you ready?"

I reply, "Yes, I've got my work clothes on."

Frank doesn't talk to me much as we are working. When my arms are about to fall off, Frank announces that it's time for lunch. We go to the canteen and have a sandwich and a glass of tea.

We head back over to the House of Boho that Cindy and Frank live in. I guess Frank decided they should get their windows done first since he is heading up this project. As we finish, Frank tells me we are headed to the House of Blood. Thinking about my experience there makes me shudder. Aren't there bad things in there? My brainwashing has made me forget so many things.

Frank says, "The House of Blood is so spiritual. The blood of Jesus saved our souls. Sometimes I wish I could live here."

I reply, "No, you don't. There are bad things in there. Don't ask me how I know because I can't remember. I have a bad feeling about it."

He replies, "You're crazy, girl. It's a house of Jesus's love for us."

As we finish this house, Frank walks me back to my building. "Rachael, we're done for the day. Get cleaned up. Cindy will come get you soon."

Cindy arrives about thirty minutes later and struts inside. No one knocks around here.

She says, "Did you have a good day?"

"Yes, I cleaned the windows of two buildings today. It was hard work, but I don't mind. Work is good for your body and mind. However, I really don't have a choice."

"Well, you have many more buildings to work on. Frank told me that you will be working with him for the rest of this week."

"Oh, boy," I say.

After dinner, Jerry walks me back to my building. He kisses me briefly and says, "Sweet dreams!"

In my bed, I think about my purpose in the commune. I guess my purpose is to worship God, do my chores, and obey the rules. Obedience is the number one rule here. How do I get myself into so much trouble? As I drift off to sleep, I remember how lucky I am to be here.

I feel like I'm floating. I think it is a cloud. Will I finally get to go to heaven? I'm floating down our river on an inner tube. I feel so peaceful as I drift slowly down the river. I get to the shallow part and see Harold playing with a mouse. I float past him and see my two friends playing. Harold grabs me and tries to stab me. He is actually stabbing the mouse, and I continue floating down the river.

All of a sudden, I'm floating with Joe and Veronica on our inner tubes. We jump in the water and splash each other. As we jump back on our inner tubes, I see Gary. He waves to me. I wave back. He is smiling at me. I look around to see if Harold is around, but I just see all my friends having fun in the river. I am having a blast.

I wake up and wonder if I just had a good dream for once. I then hear someone knocking on my door. Is it daylight already?

Frank is coming to get me to eat before we start our washing windows.

I say, "I'll be ready in a minute."

He replies, "OK. You can't oversleep this week. We have a lot of work to do."

I get up and put on my work clothes. "I'll do better tomorrow. I had a horrible dream about a murderer named Harold. He stabbed me and then a mouse. Have Leader Charles and Jerry told you about my night terrors? They are horrible."

Frank says, "Rachael, this place is dangerous—and someone might be watching us out in the woods."

I reply, "Who?"

"You know how the biker gang came by here, and there's no telling who might be investigating us. You need to be ready at all times."

"What do you mean?"

"Never mind. Don't say anything about the woods. They are dangerous."

"OK, I won't." I know he would get into trouble if I said anything.

Frank leads me to the House of Torture, but he tells me that we are cleaning the "House of Isolation." I don't care what they call it; it has torture in there. As we are cleaning the windows, I start scanning the woods. I wonder who is out there. It could be clowns, wolves, bad guys, or even Harold out there. I don't dare ask Frank about who is watching us. I think he just wants me to be aware. What does he want me to be ready for?

We head over to the House of Power. This is where Leader Charles lives. I've been there, and it makes me sick to my stomach. Some bad things happened to me in there. He raped me and beat me in there, and I nearly died. His rage and madness were severe.

I say, "This is a bad place."

Frank replies, "No, it is not. Leader Charles lives here. He is our fearless leader, and he loves God and us so much. We're going over to the House of Peace for our final windows of the day. I know you are tired, but we have to finish all of them by the end of the week."

"I'm ready. This is where Jerry and I lived for a while. We had fun and got to know one another. It was peaceful for me. But it didn't stop my horrible dreams. I ended up sleeping on the couch, and then Jerry moved out. It wasn't so peaceful for us in the end. Jerry beat me just like Leader Charles did. I guess I didn't follow the rules, and I had it coming."

Frank looks at me funny, but he doesn't say anything.

We work as fast as we can, and it is so hot. I really need something to drink.

Frank walks me back to my building and says, "Someone will come to get you for dinner soon."

CHAPTER FORTY
SPENCER'S INFORMATION

Spencer enters the police department and asks to talk to Officer Dale.

Officer Dale comes out to the lobby with his notebook. He always writes down everything.

As they walk back to Officer Dale's office, Spencer says, "I checked through my old patient files and Rachael's files again. Both patients talk about the followers there. They also talked about the leader and called him Leader Charles. I ran a background check and found out he was the leader of a commune near Laredo for ten years. He went there from Utah. Can you run a background check to see if he has ever been in prison?"

"Spencer, do you have a last name for him?"

"When I googled 'Leader Charles, commune in West Texas,' it came up with a picture of him and said his name was Charles Wayne Hinson. I hope this helps."

Officer Dale laughs and says, "Well, we finally have a good lead. I will notify all the authorities immediately. I will also tell Gary that we have something to go on. Thank you, Spencer! We will catch this dirty rat."

Spencer says, "I hope you catch him. He's not a good Christian man."

Officer Dale looks at him funny and says, "Spencer, how do you know this? Have you met this guy or been to the commune?"

Spencer says, "No, no, I don't know him. I'm just saying that I bet he is bad."

Officer Dale is very suspicious of Spencer. After he calls the authorities, he calls Gary and says, "We have a lead!"

Gary replies, "Oh my goodness, what is going on? Did you find Rachael?"

"No, but we have a good lead. I can't go into much detail, but Spencer was able to give us some information that will lead us to them. We will get your Rachael back as soon as we can. I promise you."

"OK, just keep me informed. I hope she is not hurt. Please save my wife."

"We will do the best we can. Please call her parents and give them the good news. It's not over yet, but we are getting close."

"I will call them right now." Gary calls Rachael's parents and says, "Well, the police have a good lead now. They will find Rachael. Just pray that it happens soon."

Irene asks, "What is it? Do they know what town she is in?"

Gary says, "I don't know all the details, but her therapist told them about the leader of the commune and where it is located. They are working to find her."

Dad says, "Thank goodness. I hope they find my daughter soon. I'm so worried."

Mama starts crying and says, "I have not been sleeping for a long time. I hope they find her soon—and I hope she is all right."

CHAPTER FORTY-ONE
EVIL SÉANCE

Cindy walks me to the canteen and says, "Girl, we're going to have fun tonight. At worship, there is going to be a séance for you. We will all be laying hands on you and praying for you. We also will try to contact the dead, and Leader Charles will be our medium. You know he talks to the dead, right?"

"What dead person is Leader Charles going to talk to? How does that relate to me?"

Cindy says, "He is going to try to bring up the biggest fear in your life. He is going to bring Harold back to talk to you."

"I don't want to talk to Harold. I hate him. How do you guys know so much about Harold? I guess I talk too much in my sleep."

She says, "Yep, we know all about Harold. We are convinced that your nightmares will be over if you just face your fear. That guy did a trip on you for sure."

I don't say another word as we eat. The food is always good and healthy. Why are Leader Charles and Jerry confiding in Cindy so much? Is it because they know I'm close to her? What in the world is going to happen to me today?

Cindy gets up from the table and says, "Get up, girl. It's showtime!"

In the chapel, there are candles everywhere. Even with the candles, it's very scary and dark. Cindy leads me to the front and sits me in a chair. I wonder who put her in charge?

Everyone is staring at me like I'm a freak or something.

Leader Charles walks up to me and places his hand on my head. "This is a spiritual meeting to receive spirit communication. We are here tonight to make contact with Harold's spirit. Harold, please come and talk to Rachael. Tell her that you are all right—and her friends are all right too. Everyone, please chant with me. Harold, come forth. Harold, come forth."

The followers repeat it over and over.

A loud noise shakes the windows of the chapel.

I scream, "Go away, Harold. I don't need you!"

The followers keep chanting.

I hang my head and start crying.

All is quiet except my whimpers. I'm so scared that I will see Harold's face.

Something hits the windows again.

Leader Charles says, "Harold has come to visit Rachael. Rachael, he is standing before you asking for forgiveness. Do you see him, Rachael?"

I reply, "Yes, I heard something outside the window. Is he there?"

Leader Charles replies, "He is sorry that he has tormented you all these years. He is living in hell because of his unforgiven sins. However, he wants you to know that you are now free from him and his fear in your mind. He says you are now free to go on with your life without the night terrors."

I say, "Thank you so much, Leader Charles. I feel so good now. I am free from the worry and sin of my dreams. Thank you for saving me."

As I stand up, all the followers start clapping. They file out and sing "I'm Redeemed." I feel better about Harold. Maybe he did visit and is sorry for what he did. His father, Johnny, tormented him his whole life and made him kill people. Johnny is as much to blame as Harold. Johnny is a horrible man also. Maybe he just wants me to know that he is sorry—and now I can go on with my life without being afraid.

Cindy and Frank meet me at the back of the church and walk me to my building.

Frank says, "Rachael, I'll see you in the morning."

I'm so tired, but I start thinking about what occurred in the chapel. Do these people think Harold really came to see me? I don't know if he did or not. I don't want to see him ever again. Did I really see him?

As I drift off to sleep, I start dreaming.

I'm sitting in this chair, and there are demons all around me. Harold walks up to me with a mouse in his hand. I start to scream, but he puts his hand over my mouth.

Mama and Dad walk into the back of the church and start singing.

My brother is leading the music.

Everyone is so happy, but then they start chanting, "Harold, kill her. Harold, kill her."

I look around for something because I need to kill him before he murders me. I grab a knife, but he grabs it and shakes it out of my hand. I scream as he slashes my throat.

I'm not dead. I'm always running from something. A small person in a black hoodie is chasing me. The person has a large spider in their hand. I can see it; it is brown. I am sure it is a brown recluse. That is the bad kind. It is very poisonous. The little person screams,

"I'm going to get you and kill you!" Under the black hoodie, there is long brown hair. As they come near to me, they throw the spider at me. I scream.

Frank walks in and yells, "Be quiet, Rachael, before someone hears you. You know what they will do to you if they hear you scream."

"I know. I'll be ready in a minute." I'm so thankful that Frank doesn't beat me and rape me every time he catches me dreaming and screaming. Maybe Frank is a good guy. I get ready quickly, and we eat and go to work.

We go to the House of Happiness. I guess Frank thinks I need to get the bad things out of my mind. Why did this commune give all these buildings different names? Some of the names are cute, but some of them have bad things going on. The windows are decorated with emojis of happy faces, funny faces, and smiling faces. The artwork makes me smile. Who could have thought of this? I guess the followers are creative and came up with all this stuff.

This house is just amazing. I wash the windows and think about the séance. It was not a spiritual session. It was evil. Trying to bring up Harold is the worst thing in the world for them to do. Leader Charles and Jerry have no clue what will help me, but neither do I.

CHAPTER FORTY-TWO
THE BEAT GOES ON

Frank takes me to the House of Love. I look in the window, and I see a room with pillows all over the floor. It looks so comfortable in there. Many people can sit down and talk. They are four beds in this house, and I wonder if orgies go on in the building. I wash the windows, and I don't say a word to Frank about what I think this building is used for.

We then go to the House of Fear. Who would live in this building? I don't even look in the windows. I just keep washing them. My imagination is going wild. I think there are spiders and snakes in there. There are probably spooky cowboys in there also. I think they have monsters in there too. My imagination is off the wall. I'm glad I never had to live in this one.

"Frank, why is this place called the House of Fear? What goes on in this building?"

He replies, "I don't know, but make sure they don't put you in there. It will be worse than those scary movies they are making you watch."

"I know I'm in the House of Isolation, but I think it should be called the House of Torture. I don't want to live in this one at all."

"Rachael, please watch out for yourself. All kinds of things are possible in this commune. Go on and be happy here—and don't worry about all the buildings. You are curious and want to check things out. This is what gets you in trouble—along with the bad dreams.

"I like to figure out things and investigate. This is how I get myself into messes. Do you ever wonder if this is a good place or not? I've seen some things that go on here, but I can't remember what they are. I know bad things happen in the House of Blood. Have you seen anything?"

"Rachael, keep your nose out of things. You always get caught. The Bible says, 'Be sure your sins will find you out.' That's the reason you always get caught."

"I don't believe I'm sinning. All I'm trying to do is find out what's going on here. I can't help the night terrors and screams. Maybe they are being too rough on me here. This place is sometimes good and happy, but some bad things go on here."

Frank replies, "Just stay out of things, and you will be better off."

"How can I stop dreaming?"

"I don't know, Rachael. Just remember that you are a child of God, and he takes away the bad things in our lives. However, you must work in good faith to do good."

We finish quickly, and Frank says, "We're done for the day. There are more buildings on this campus, but we're not allowed to go near them. The large quarters where the majority of our followers sleep will be tomorrow, and then we will be done."

What other types of buildings could there be? Maybe the House of Death where they kill people? I try to stop myself from thinking that way. I remember the movie. This is a happy place, and I'm lucky to live here. Everyone is so nice to me, and they are so happy.

Frank walks me to my building and says, "Rachael, you will not be allowed to eat in the canteen tonight."

"Why not?"

"Someone heard you screaming. You have to be punished for this. I'm sorry, but I can't do anything about it."

Did Frank tell them?

I sit down and wait to find out how bad the punishment will be—and who will be handing it out.

Jerry walks into my building and says, "Rachael, you have done it again. You have broken a rule again—and now you have to be punished. This time, I'm going to make a believer out of you."

He slaps my face, and I drop to my knees. Oh gosh, I've gotten myself into another mess.

He picks me up, removes my clothes, and ties me to the bed. He removes his clothes, and I see a cross in his hand. I cry out in fear as he slaps me again and beats me with his fist. He lifts the cross. "In the name of Jesus, demons, come out of her." He inserts the cross deep into my vagina.

I feel my skin ripping inside of me. I am crying loudly.

He slaps me again and tells me to be quiet—or he won't stop.

I make myself shut up.

He gets out of my bed and dresses. "Rachael, this had to be done because some of the followers heard you screaming last night. You had to be punished—or this will never stop. Harold is gone, and you need to realize that and get over the night terrors. I will be putting you on the table. You will sleep there tonight and watch the scary movies. Something needs to snap in your brain, and you need to realize that these bad dreams are ridiculous." He carries me to the table and straps me down.

I can't believe the beatings are still going on. I thought I saw kindness in Jerry and that he did not totally agree with Leader Charles. I now know that Jerry is unkind, and he is obedient to Leader Charles. I must never think anyone is on my side here.

As Jerry walks out, he says, "Rachael, we are going to wear you down one way or the other. Watch the movies. I hope they drive the fear out of your mind."

I shiver on the table, naked and afraid, and I say, "I'm sorry, Jerry. It won't happen again."

I watch the spider movie again. I hate spiders. I used to kill them if my husband wasn't home. What is my husband's name? I can't remember, but at least I remember that I had one. He was a good man, and he went to work every day to support our family. I try to ignore the movie and think good thoughts as I drift into another dream.

Gary is having an affair with Carol, and I see them kissing. I watch as they run down to the river. I follow them, and then I see Harold. Of course, Harold is just watching them too. Harold kills Ryan and Sarah again. I just stand there watching my husband and Carol kissing, and then Harold murders the kids again. Blood is rolling down the hill and flowing into the river. The river is bright red and then I see the knife in my hand. Who did I kill?

Gary is running toward me. I am smiling because I know he is coming for me. I am sure he still loves me. He turns away and starts running toward Anne. She is standing over by a tree, and she is smiling at him. He stops and glances at me, and then he glances at Anne. I think he is trying to decide between us. I run toward him as tears roll down my face. As I get closer, he is smiling, but he is not smiling at me. He is smiling at Anne.

I start talking to Gary in Harold and Johnny's house. He says that Anne is his girl—and that I need to go away. I see her laughing at me, and there is so much evil coming out of her. She chases me down a very long hall, and I can see the knife in her hand. I keep running and running for my life, and she just keeps laughing.

As I wake up, I think about how I am such a jealous person. Why is Gary going after other women—and not just me?

CHAPTER FORTY-THREE
LOVE AND MARRIAGE

Cindy walks into my building in the morning. She unstraps me from the table and helps me to my bathroom. I wonder if she has done this before for other girls at the commune. She acts like it's no big deal that I have been beaten and raped and tied to that awful table all night.

My body is so sore, and I stretch to make it feel better. As I am cleaning myself and getting dressed, Cindy is humming like she is the happiest girl in the world. She walks into the bathroom and starts putting the salve on my back. It numbs things and makes my back feel so much better. I wonder how Cindy can fit in here so well and be so happy.

As we are walking to breakfast, she says, "Frank and I are going to get married. Do you want to stand up with me?"

I am shocked. "Really? You're getting married so soon. I guess they will let me stand up with you. I hope so. I think you will be a beautiful bride. Are you sure you really know him? You have to know that you are equally yoked like the Bible says."

She replies, "Of course we are equally yoked. We are very compatible with each other. He is my soul mate—plus he is so good in bed."

"Cindy, you're not supposed to have sex before marriage!"

"Rachael, you are so old-fashioned. People have sex all the time before marriage."

"Yep, and that's the reason for so many failed marriages. You don't even know him before you start sleeping with him. Of course, he falls for you when you are giving him some. You really don't know him, and he doesn't know you. When you really get to know him by living with him, you might find out some things you don't like about him. Then you are stuck like chuck with him."

"That's good advice, Rachael, but I've already blown it. I really want to marry him."

Cindy continues talking about Frank and how much she loves him. She said the same thing about Bill. Why is Cindy so naïve and dumb?

We get our food and walk over to an empty table. My bottom hurts so much. I am glad to have the salve and will use it again tonight. Luckily, Jerry only slapped me in the face and didn't leave any bruises on me. Leader Charles left some bruises, but they are hidden under my clothes. I try to focus on what Cindy is saying.

"Yes, and then I will have all colors of flowers in my wedding. Frank is going to build a small archway for me. It's going to look like a rainbow. Our dresses will be lovely, don't you think?"

"What did you say they will look like?"

"You weren't listening to me, girl. Our dresses will be bohemian and colorful. Bettye can sew really good, and she is going to help make them. She is going to use material from our clothes storage room. No one will be wearing shoes. We will have flowers in our hair. It's going to be beautiful!"

Frank walks in and says, "What's beautiful?"

Cindy shouts, "Our wedding, honey!"

He says, "Yes, it will be, Cindy. Rachael, are you ready to go to work?"

I reply, "Yes, but I may be a bit slow today. I'm not feeling very good."

He says, "That's OK. We only have to do the large quarters. It won't be too bad. I'll work harder so that you won't have to. Let's go!"

I get up and follow him. Each step hurts. This place is wicked!

As we are washing the windows, Frank says, "Rachael, I know you are getting raped and beaten—and I don't believe that is right. I don't believe that is the cure for you. I know you need professional help with all your night terrors. I know that some of the punishments are because you ran away. Please don't try that again."

"I know I need help. The help they are giving me is about to kill me. This is outrageous."

"Rachael, never repeat anything I say. If Leader Charles and Jerry find out that I'm talking to you, they will kill me."

"Oh my gosh. You are kidding, right?"

"Nope, I'm not kidding." He continues to wash windows.

My mind is everywhere. Are people getting killed here? I guess I'm lucky for my punishment. At least I'm still alive. I wish I could remember my past. Everything is so foggy. All I remember is this commune and that I'm supposed to be very happy here. All the followers seem happy. I can be happy here too. This is all I know.

Frank walks me back to my building. I hate this house. What kind of lesson is God trying to teach me? I've always heard that we go through things for a reason, a season, or a lifetime. What am I going through? I hope it's just for a season. I hope the rapes, beatings, torture, and punishments stop soon. I need to focus on being good and obeying every rule. That way, I will stay out of trouble.

Jerry walks into my building and says, "Rachael, hurry up and get ready for dinner. We are having a dinner in honor of Frank and Cindy. I know you will enjoy it so much."

I reply, "I'm excited for them. Just give me a few minutes."

Jerry and I walk hand in hand to the canteen. We will be going to worship after dinner so that Frank and Cindy can be blessed for their future together.

CHAPTER FORTY-FOUR
WEDDING DAY

I'm all healed up from my last ordeal and feel much better. I have been doing chores, going to meals in the canteen, and worshipping with everyone. We are getting ready for Cindy's wedding. Bettye has sewn our dresses out of colorful materials that she saved or found in the clothing room. We will look like fairies and gypsies with our dresses and flowers.

Tomorrow is the big day, and Cindy is so excited. Frank seems nervous, and he has been very quiet. I stay away from Frank. I don't want anyone—namely Leader Charles and Jerry—to think I have gotten close to Frank. I've got to keep my nose clean around here in order to stay out of trouble. If I mess up, I am punished to the hilt. This place is so strict, and I can't get away with anything.

One of the followers has a black eye. I wonder what he did. He probably screwed up his chores. Maybe he was too slow … or he did something really bad. Perhaps he talked back to Leader Charles or Jerry. If you do that around here, you'll get in horrible trouble.

Jerry walks over and says, "Rachael, can I walk you to worship?"

I say, "Of course you can. I have no other choice, right?"

Jerry replies, "Rachael, don't be mad at me. You brought it on yourself."

"I guess."

I am in a better mood at worship. The music is so good, and everyone sings "Celebrate Me Home." It's such a good song about going to heaven. Everyone starts clapping as an upbeat song is played. I don't know all the words yet, but the other followers do. They are so joyous and happy. I wish I could totally get into the groove here. Maybe I would be happier if my punishments stopped. Will I ever stay out of trouble?

After the service, Jerry walks me to my building. "Rachael, you will soon be moving into my building."

"Jerry, I still have bad feelings toward you because of my last rape and beatings."

Why does he do that to me? I thought he loved me. I have no choice about where I live. All I need to do is work on not dreaming and screaming. I will do just fine with him. I love that house. It is so peaceful in there. I actually love this commune, and the followers are so happy here. I need to be good and run from my struggles.

Jerry says, "Rachael, you have to be punished when you break the rules. That's just the way it is around here."

"I know all about the rules. I seem to break them all the time. When will I get out of trouble around here? I'm not sure how much longer I can take all the rough treatment that is handed out to me."

"You will be just fine, Rachael. Moving back with me will calm your nerves. I believe you have had enough alone time. Just stop all the nonsense with those bad dreams, and you will be fine."

"Jerry, have you ever gotten in trouble here?"

"Yes, when I first came here with no place to go, I thought I was a badass. I decided to buck up to Leader Charles and tell him the rules were too strict here. I wanted to smoke marijuana, but it wasn't allowed. I brought some with me, but it was taken away immediately. Only privileged followers are allowed to do that here."

I ask, "Did you get beaten?"

"I don't want to talk about it. Let's just say I almost didn't live to tell you about this. Don't you dare tell anyone what I have told you. I'm a good follower now and have made it up to second-in-command. I've done good here."

I reply, "I guess you did."

He drops me off at the door and gives me a small kiss. I walk into my living nightmare building and wonder what else is going to happen to me. The things they do to people to get them to be obedient followers can't be legal. I know they beat, rape, perform illegal abortions, and do lots of other things that are not legal. What else do they do around here? I wonder if anyone has died here. Jerry did say that he almost didn't live. What kind of place is this?

I was driving down the road with Cindy and she started bleeding out of her nose. I asked her what was wrong. She looked at me and I saw buttons over her eyes. She had a knife in her hand and started stabbing me in my legs. I screamed and then she stopped. She then acted like nothing was wrong and started talking to me again. As we got out of her car, my legs were just fine. Then I saw Leader Charles and I ran away from him as far as I could go. I was running into these woods trying to escape.

I'm then at a hotel resort and there are people swimming in the pool. I see Cindy is there. One of my boys, who looked about four years old, walked over to this guy in this cubicle type area, and he smiled at my son. I immediately told him to not touch my boy. Cindy started flirting with him. Then, everyone starts eating at this large brunch. I needed to go to work and was leaving. As I was leaving, I jumped into the pool in my clothes. I just wanted to have fun before I left.

When I wake up the next morning, I remember my weird dreams from the night before. What a hodgepodge of dreams they were.

It's Cindy's wedding day. We will have so much fun celebrating with them. I love the thought of being married and having a family of my own. I hope my wished-for family doesn't come from Leader Charles. He has raped me so many times, and I fear having his child. I get dressed and walk to the canteen by myself for the first time. I feel such freedom today.

I see Cindy and Frank, and everyone is standing around them. People are praying over them and asking God for peace and love in their life. I grab someone's hand and join in with the prayers. I'm still an outsider here, but most of the followers do not shunt me at all now.

After the prayer, I whispered to Cindy, "I thought you're not supposed to see each other on your wedding day? Isn't that bad luck?"

Cindy says, "Frank couldn't stand not seeing me this morning. Leader Charles told us there would be prayer for us today. Besides, I don't believe in that. I think it's an old wives' tale. Let's go decorate and get ready for my wedding. I'm so excited!"

Just like at my wedding to Jerry, we put flowers and greenery on the arch. Silver, yellow, plum, and pink flowers are everywhere. It is such a bohemian wedding. There are soft and romantic boho-chic decorations in the trees and bushes. Bettye made small lanterns, and we hang them from the trees. We use the colorful mats from my wedding, and after we finish decorating, we go to Cindy's building to help her get dressed.

Cindy's dress is so colorful and beautiful. Bettye found flowing lace and other fabrics for her. I have never seen a more beautiful dress. One of the followers had experience with fixing hair, and she fixes Cindy's hair. It is flowing down her back, and colorful flowers are pinned on her lovely silk veil. I am her maid of honor, and Jerry is the best man. I wear a bright bohemian dress, and Jerry wears a colorful vest. We are all so festive and ready for their wedding.

As the sun is about to set, Leader Charles says, "Frank and Jerry, please hold hands. We come here today to join two hearts together. God, you have created us in the image of love. Bless those who stand before you."

They exchange vows, and Leader Charles announces them as husband and wife. As they kiss, all the followers clap. It is a happy day at the commune. The reception is so much fun, and there is dancing all night long. After the married couple's first dance, Jerry and I dance with them. Since Cindy's father isn't there, she dances with Leader Charles—just like I did when I married Jerry. I wonder if she feels weird dancing with him like I did. She is smiling and laughing with him. The music is so great, and everyone is happy and having fun.

We all eat cake and drank wine and punch. Everyone is dancing, laughing, and getting drunk.

Cindy throws her bouquet, and one of the single followers catches it. She tries to get me to catch it, but I tell her that I am still married to Jerry.

She says, "Oh, that's right, I forgot about that after you ran away."

The wedding is so much fun.

Jerry is dancing with me, and he tells me that I will be moving in with him on Monday morning. Maybe it will work for us this time. I love this commune. Maybe I won't have to go back to the House of Isolation. It is such a torture house. Everything would be perfect if I stopped dreaming.

When the wedding celebration ends, we all go back to our buildings.

I am so tired, and my feet hurt. I don't dream at first, and I am so thankful. I guess I am just tired. Then my nightmares return.

Anne was holding John and James in front of me. She dropped them into this burning fire in their backyard. I ran and grabbed them, and they were not burned at all. I looked over at her and pushed her into the fire. I could see her long brown hair burning. She screamed but was not burning at all. I remembered thinking, that's unbelievable. I grabbed a knife and stabbed her in the heart, but it did not kill her. She just laughed at me, and then I knew she was a devil and not of this world.

I awake, shaking, of course, but remembering things from my past. My dreams are getting weird to say the least.

In the morning, Cook takes me to the canteen. I thought I was going to be able to walk by myself again. I guess their trust in me just goes so far.

Cindy and Frank don't have to work for a week. Everyone is calling them lovebirds, which happened when Jerry and I got married.

Cook says, "Wasn't that a lovely wedding?"

"Yes, it was. Everything was so beautiful. Do they have many weddings here? I've only seen mine and Cindy's now."

"I've seen a few other weddings. Most of the followers here are already married when they arrive. Leader Charles really likes people to be equally yoked so there will be much harmony here. He doesn't like it when people like you are here. I don't think he is a bad man, but he is a stern man. He does not tolerate disobedience. Are you starting to understand that?"

"Yes, ma'am. I get the picture. I've had so much torment since I came back. I ran away from this place because I have another family."

"I thought you didn't remember any of your past?"

"Well, I really don't remember much of my old life. I have a few ideas in my head of what it used to be like. Cook, I like it here now. I do not plan on running away again. I love Jerry, and I'm going to move back in with him. I feel pretty lucky."

"Well, you better behave. Don't forget what was done to you."

CHAPTER FORTY-FIVE
MOVING IN WITH JERRY

In the morning, I am so happy that my bad dreams have decreased. Maybe the torture, brainwashing, and scary movies messed up my brain and made me have more horrendous dreams. The rapes and beatings caused so much trauma in my mind. I think I'm getting better now. I've had night terrors since I was a little girl, and all that nonsense should be behind me. Who am I kidding?

I'm moving today! It is so exciting to get out of this place. I know I can be good and obey all the rules. I need to calm down at night to prevent the bad dreams. I'm going to tell Jerry that I want to start meditation and yoga classes. I believe they will help with my stress and anxiety. I believe these classes will help me. I've got my hopes up so high. I kind of remember that I used to attend group classes. I remember a bunch of ladies, and we all talked about our issues at sessions. I hope they will let me go to some of the classes. I know they will help me.

After I bring my few over to Jerry's house, we walk to the canteen. Why did I run away? Isn't this a lovely place to live?

"Jerry, I'm so excited to get to live with you again. I know you're my soul mate. I know you did some bad things to me, but Leader Charles made you do it. You were just following orders, right?"

Jerry replies, "I do follow the rules around here. That's something you do not do. I love you, but I also know what you are capable of doing. I will keep a close watch on you. These good people at this commune are just here to be happy and love the Lord. You need to do the same."

"I will. I've learned my lesson. I know you're really a good guy. You just like to act tough."

"I am tough—and don't you forget it. I will do whatever it takes to control you."

"I know you will. I don't care about that. I'm going to love you to death because you are my true love. I also love this commune. Everyone is so nice to me. I promise not to break any rules around here."

"I hope so. I don't like the punishments that I have to do to you. At least I know you are a very strong woman. You can take a lot."

"Let's go to breakfast now and then go to worship."

Jerry is working in the garden this week, and I'm working in the kitchen with Cook. I'm so excited to be learning how to cook.

Cook looks up and says, "Well, if it isn't my meal prep girl!"

"Yes, ma'am," I reply with a smile.

"Come over here, and I will get you started on our dinner tonight."

I help her with the preparation of the vegetables and make a salad. I used to be good at that.

"Rachael, do you mind washing some pots and pans before we finish the meal? It will make it so easy for me after dinner."

I reply, "Yes, of course."

As I'm washing dishes, I think about my night with Jerry. After washing all the dishes, I sweep and mop the floor. I want to be very tired tonight because I don't dream very much when I'm tired. I will be sure to keep Jerry busy in bed tonight too. I want him to go into a deep sleep—so I don't wake him up if I have any night terrors. Afterward, I will sleep on the couch. I know he has to work, and I don't want him getting mad at me. I fear the beatings from Jerry and Leader Charles. They will not tolerate my screaming.

Jerry comes to the kitchen and says, "We are going home early today—before dinner. I need you badly, and it is not out of anger."

I reply, "That sounds good to me."

Cook waves goodbye, and we walk toward our building. I'm very excited to make tender love with Jerry. I don't want to have the horrible sexual madness that occurred in the torture house. I hope Jerry is gentle with me.

We make love slowly, and Jerry tells me that he still loves me. He never apologizes about the beatings and rapes. I know he was very angry with me at the time and just flew into a rage. Leader Charles made him torture me. Jerry was just obeying the authority figure in his life.

Leader Charles has the ability to make anyone dispense horrible punishments. I wonder what type of criminal he was in his past life. I'm sure he has been in prison. He's too evil to stop doing unlawful things. Jerry was just being obedient to his superior. What a horrible person Leader Charles is. Will I ever be able to stay out of trouble?

Our lovemaking is nice and sensual. Afterward, we get dressed for dinner. We will be having worship tonight, and I'm excited about that.

As we walk to the canteen, Jerry says, "Rachael, never forget that I love you. You must forget your past—and things will be good for you here. This is a good place to live."

"I will never forget the punishments. I will never run away again. I'm still sorry for that."

"I'm just happy you are back. I missed you while you were gone. I love you, Rachael, with all my heart. I kept Leader Charles from killing you. Never forget that."

"I will never forget that, Jerry. I owe you my life."

After dinner, we go to the chapel for Worship Night. Jerry is holding my hand and is very happy. We are singing and shouting to the Lord. Everything is so perfect here. Jerry loves me again, and I'm worshipping with him and all my friends.

Leader Charles speaks about obedience to the Lord and to the leaders of our commune. I know he is talking to me. I guess he thinks he has to beat it into my head. He reads Deuteronomy 11:26–28 from the King James Version:

Behold, I set before you this day a blessing and a curse; A blessing, if ye obey the commandments of the Lord your God, which I command you this day: And a curse, if ye will not obey the commandments of the Lord your God, but turn aside out of the way which I command you this day, to go after other gods, which ye have not known.

After reading the scripture, he says, "You know that means that you have to obey all the rules; otherwise, you will be cursed. You do not want to be cursed by God. You do not want to be cursed by my authority either. I am a man of God, and he instructs me on the ways that our commune should be. Our commune is doing great acts of the Lord. We are a chosen people, and we are strong. I will lead you in the ways that have been sent to me in my dreams. These are dreams from God, and he talks to me every day. I am his chosen one, and I sit with him with the Trinity. I am the One."

As I sit there, I remember my old Christian background. What little I can remember, thanks to the brainwashing, is that what Leader Charles is saying is bull. I do not believe he is telling us the truth.

As we walk to our building, I ask Jerry if he liked the sermon.

Jerry replies, "It was fine."

After we make love again, I go to the couch. He doesn't stop me. He knows I don't want to get in trouble again. He also knows that he needs sleep.

I'm on the couch, and I am trying very hard to stay awake. I don't want to dream. I don't want to be beaten again. Jerry has all that rage and anger in him, and I know what he is capable of doing. I know he will tell on me to Leader Charles because he is very loyal to him. I love him, but I'm so leery of him. He and Leader Charles can be monsters.

I drift off to sleep.

A man is walking toward me. He wears glasses and looks like Poindexter. The nerd continues coming toward me, and his face is turning red. I stare at him, and a small girl walks up beside him. Her name is Anne. She is a bad girl who did something with Harold. Her face turns red, and she runs away. Spencer is just staring at me. Who is this guy?

I am hanging people with a very large rope. The rope is so thick. There are so many people dying. At some point, someone finds out what I am doing. They are going to hang me. I am working in a church, for some reason, and then I see the rope hanging down from a rafter that is going to be used on me. I remember eating with many people, and I am trying to avoid being hung. The rope is swinging back and forth.

What a strange dream. I wake up on Jerry's couch. I don't scream, but I'm confused about all the people in my dream. I need to remember all these people. They have to be people from my past. I rack my brain, but I don't remember much from my past. All the brainwashing has made my brain foggy.

I get up and get a spiral notebook from the kitchen. I make notes about my dreams and the people in them. I need to figure this out, and I need to find a hiding place for this notebook. I don't want anyone to find it. I've got to keep it secret to avoid more torture.

CHAPTER FORTY-SIX

MORNING SICKNESS

As I get up for my day in the kitchen, I run to the bathroom and vomit.

Jerry comes up to the door and says, "Rachael, are you OK?"

I reply, "Yes, I must have eaten something that didn't sit well with me last night."

Jerry says, "Well, I hope you are not coming down with a virus. I love you, Rachael, but I don't want to get it. It would be terrible for me. I'd probably have diarrhea so bad. I don't want that for sure. Come on. Let's go eat."

I hope I'm not pregnant. Why did I immediately think this? Between Leader Charles and Jerry, I couldn't even guess who the father is. It would be impossible to know. This predicament crossed my mind when they were raping me. I certainly did not consent to it. Maybe I did eat something that didn't agree with me. I hope that is the reason for the nausea and vomiting. I feel so lousy and want to lay in bed, but I go to breakfast. I know what is expected of me.

As we stand in line, I don't feel well. I get my normal coffee, which is always so good, and a couple of pieces of toast. I hope I can hold this down. Lord, please don't let me be pregnant. Tomorrow will be a better day.

Frank and Cindy are holding hands as they walk into the canteen.

Cindy says, "We're having so much fun on our honeymoon ... if you know what I mean. Getting to sleep late is like heaven on earth. How are you guys?"

Jerry says, "We're fine. Rachael slept good last night with no dreams. We're having fun also ... if you know what I mean!"

At the same time, Cindy and Frank say, "We do know!"

I roll my eyes, and a wave of nausea hits me. I try to not make it too obvious, but I walk to the bathroom as fast as I can. I'm so worried about pregnancy, especially around here. There are no children here. Why don't the followers have children? What is the deal?

Jerry walks me back to our building, and I lay down.

He says, "You don't have to go to work this morning, but after lunch, go to the kitchen and help Cook with our dinner."

I reply weakly, "I will, but just let me lie down again. This nausea is horrible. I don't like it."

He walks toward the door and says, "I'm going to the garden to work. You know I'm the best at gardening. I'll see you tonight and walk with you to dinner. I hope you feel better."

I reply, "Oh, I will. All this sickness will pass. It's just a virus."

Why are there no children in this commune? Everyone is so happy here. I would think there would be children running and playing everywhere. Is it a rule that no babies can be born here? Why doesn't Leader Charles like children? I run to the bathroom and vomit again. I feel so bad, and I stay in bed.

At noon, I get up and feel much better. I hope this is just a twenty-four-hour virus. I hate this feeling and all the vomiting. I walk to the kitchen to help with dinner.

Cook looks at me and says, "Rachael, are you feeling better? You look pretty rough. Is Jerry being nice to you?"

I reply, "Oh, yes, he is. I think I have some type of stomach virus—or I ate something last night that didn't agree with me."

She says, "I don't think anything I prepare would make you sick. I'm very clean and wash everything before it is prepared. I don't leave anything out on the counter. It is all refrigerated. I hope a virus is all it is. Now wash your hands good and start prepping the vegetables for me."

"Yes, ma'am. Our vegetables from the garden are so good. I know they keep us so healthy. I don't know why I'm nauseous."

Cook looks at me funny and says, "Let me know if it keeps up. I can make a green tea that will settle your stomach."

I hope something works. Does Cook know I'm pregnant? For heaven's sake, it's only been one morning.

I wash the dishes and look out the window. I see a stranger walking into the House of Blood with Leader Charles. Who is she?

Jerry meets me at the canteen for dinner. When he walks in, my heart takes a leap. I'm so glad to see him. I know he loves me so much. I just want to fit in here and be happy with all the followers. I love this commune and all the happy people.

Jerry kisses me and says, "How are you feeling?"

"I feel great. I hope it was just a twenty-four-hour bug. How are you doing?"

"If you are eating good, you can thank me and my crew. We work so hard in the garden. We have about two acres, and you will not find any weeds or bugs around. We're the best!"

I had forgotten how Jerry brags so much about himself. He certainly is proud of what he does here, and I agree: the vegetables are the best.

CHAPTER FORTY-SEVEN

STRANGERS

After dinner, Jerry and I walk to the chapel for Worship Night. I decide to not say a word about the stranger I saw. We sing and worship for a long time. I'm so happy here. I really can't remember anything before this. All the brainwashing and torture have really done a number on my brain.

We walk home, and Jerry says, "Rachael, I hope you feel better in the morning. We can't have any pregnancies around here."

I ask, "Why aren't children allowed here?"

Jerry replies, "I love children, but they just don't fit in here at our commune. They may see things they are not allowed to see. You know how children are; they are always curious. It was this way when I arrived. Leader Charles said it was also a rule at the commune in Utah. He told me it's for the best."

I ask, "What happens if there is a slipup, and someone gets pregnant. Is everyone fixed here?"

Jerry says, "Rachael, you're asking too many questions. Get ready for bed. I'm very tired. I don't want to be rude, but please sleep on the couch tonight. I need my rest."

"I understand. I know you need your rest."

On the couch, I start thinking about the stranger I saw. Who was she? Why was she going into the House of Blood? They probably have a special room in there. It is a secret place. What do they do in there?

I drift off to sleep.

I'm walking through the House of Blood, and I have a screwdriver in my hand. It has blood all over it. As I approach the locked door, I hear something inside. A woman is screaming. I use the screwdriver to unlock the door. It's the stranger. Leader Charles has something in his hand that looks like a clothes hanger. When I look closer, I see that it's not a clothes hanger. It's a medical device. There's blood all over the floor. The woman keeps screaming, and her face is racked with pain. I close the door quickly, hoping Leader Charles didn't see me.

I wake up in the middle of the night. I'm confused by my dream, but then it hits me. That is where they perform illegal abortions. I'm sure they perform them on the followers, and they also perform them for the public for money. This is one way that money is made to pay all the bills here. I had forgotten about that. I guess my memory is so vague from all the brainwashing. This is awful, but I must not speak of it to anyone. They will punish me if I ask questions about this. They will realize that I remember things that go on around here.

I find my spiral notebook and write down everything I remember from my dream about the secret door. I describe the medical device and the woman. I don't know who she is. I have never seen her before. I remember the illegal abortion room in the House of Blood. I had no memory of it before this dream. I can't tell anyone about my dreams or memories. It is extremely important that I keep these secrets. I know what Leader Charles and Jerry are capable of.

I go back to the couch and drift off to sleep again.

I see a stranger walking into the House of Blood. He has a flashlight in his hand. I look again and see that it's Spencer. Why is he here? He turns around, looks at me, and puts his finger up to his lips. He is telling me to be quiet. My brother is right behind him. Joe has a gun in his hand. My brother loves guns, and he once asked Dad if he could have one.

I am being chased toward the river again. It is a small person, but I can't see their face. It is so dark. Veronica is running toward me. Her whole face is painted olive green. It is the same color as the garage. She has been painting with Dad. Dad keeps laughing at me. The small person disappears.

I wake up and think about my weird dream. I keep dreaming about Spencer, and now I remember my brother. I have a past life, and pieces of it are coming to me in my dreams. I grab my notebook, write down everything, and hide it. I'm so glad that Jerry is still asleep. I know he needs the rest.

I get up and start to get ready for the day.

Jerry walks out of the bedroom, looking refreshed, and he is already dressed for his day.

I run to the bathroom and vomit.

Jerry comes up behind me and says, "Rachael, what is wrong with you?"

"I guess the stomach virus is taking a bit longer to go away. It's only been two days. Maybe I'll be fine tomorrow. Please go to breakfast without me. I'll go later for coffee and some toast. I'm working in the kitchen again. Cook offered to make some green tea for me."

"I hope you are better tonight because you're going to bed with me."

I smile and reply, "That sounds good, Jerry."

I walk into the kitchen, and Cook says, "Let me fix you that green tea, girl. You need toast too. You look like you have had a rough go of it."

"Thank you, Cook. I've got to confide in you. I think I could be pregnant."

Her eyes get so big. "I thought so yesterday, but I didn't say anything. You better hope you aren't. Is it Jerry's baby?"

I reply softly, "I don't know. You know how it is around here when you are in trouble. Our so-called religious leaders around here can be vicious. If I'm pregnant, it could be Leader Charles or Jerry's baby. I think I've gotten myself into deep trouble now."

Cook replies, "Honey, if you're pregnant, it will be taken care of. We don't have children around here."

Dear Jesus, please help me.

CHAPTER FORTY-EIGHT
SLEEPLESS NIGHTS

Jerry and I hold hands and walk back to the House of Peace. I feel so close to God and feel so peaceful. I love this commune and all the people here. I couldn't ask for anything better. My dreams are slowing down, and they are showing me things from my past. I wish I knew if I am pregnant.

Jerry makes love to me, and I realize he's not the first person I've had sex with. I don't remember who it was, but that man treated me much better than Jerry does. Jerry is like a robot. He does his thang, and then it is over. I clean up, and then I go to my comfy couch. I know better than to try to sleep all night with him. I don't want to get in trouble if I have a nightmare.

I certainly don't want to go back to that torture house. I can't forget that table, being choked, and having to watch those horrendous movies day in and day out. I also remember the things that happened in my bed. I never want to go back there. The House of Isolation is the worse place I've ever been. No one would believe what they did to me. The couch is not so comfortable, but I drift off to sleep.

I'm tied to a table with a rope, and Leader Charles is coming toward me with a bloody knife. His face also has blood on it. He is about to cut me, and I see Spencer again. Spencer walks up behind him to take the knife, but Leader Charles starts slicing him repeatedly. Leader Charles is so angry that he can't stop. Spencer gets up and walks over to me. His blood is dripping onto my legs. I scream as the blood starts dripping into my eyes. Spencer is a ghost, white and red all over. I wipe the blood from my eyes and see Leader Charles with the bloody knife. He is looming over me as he strikes me repeatedly in my stomach.

I scream so loud that Jerry comes running out of the bedroom. "Rachael, what the hell are you doing? You scared me to death. Is this going to start all over again?"

"No, Jerry. I promise it won't happen again. My dreams are getting so much better. I still dream, but when I wake up, I can't even remember them."

"I hope so … for your sake. I won't tell Leader Charles this time, but it will be hell to pay for me if he finds out I've hidden something from him. If he finds out—or if they get worse—it's back in the House of Isolation for you. Do you hear me?"

I reply, "Yes, I'm so sorry."

I run to the bathroom to vomit. I will ask Cindy if she has a pregnancy test or if she will get one when she goes with Frank to pick up medical supplies.

As Jerry gets ready to leave for work, he turns around and says, "Stay here until noon, and then go back to the kitchen with Cook. I hope you are not pregnant. Hell, why do I love you?"

"I hope I'm not pregnant too. I think it's a three-day virus ... and then I'll get better."

I feel so nauseous. Jerry was kind enough to bring me a wet washrag for my forehead. It does help, but I still feel very bad. How long will I be sick? If I'm pregnant, what are they going to do to me? I guess I'll have to go to the House of Blood just like the woman the other day. I assume she was getting an abortion. What the heck really goes on here? The nausea overcomes me, and I run back to the bathroom. I feel so sick. I eat a cracker on the couch. I've got to get away from this place. If I get caught, they will kill me.

CHAPTER FORTY-NINE

OFFICER DALE'S LEAD

Officer Dale finds more information about Leader Charles and the commune. He is working closely with the investigators at the Laredo Police Department. The investigators have had some dealings and problems with the commune in the past. Mostly, they said all the followers are there because they want to be. No one is forcing them to be there. The police only go out there when something comes up. Most of the time, the commune doesn't get caught doing illegal things. They are good at hiding things and keeping their noses clean. The law knows something is going on out there, but they haven't been able to get enough evidence yet. They are keeping a close watch on them since they know the commune is not squeaky-clean.

Officer Dale speaks with the main investigator, Steven Gillman, on a daily basis. He continues to be closely involved with the investigation of the criminal actions going on at the commune. "We want to shut down the commune and arrest the criminals there. Right now, we don't have enough evidence. We know they are growing marijuana there, but we haven't caught them selling it yet. We placed an undercover investigator there six months ago. Frank, that's his fake name, has been living there and posing as a follower. He will try to find enough evidence to close them down and arrest the leaders. I do not believe it is a true Christian commune doing good for people. I believe they have a secret agenda."

Steven says, "We even had a biker gang go through the commune to look for anything illegal. They were run off very quickly by the fearless leader. The leader of the biker gang saw buildings everywhere. All of them had a name on the door. One of them was the House of Blood, but they did not see anything illegal while they were there. I know we will catch them soon. Frank will find enough evidence to close it down and put a lot of crooks in jail."

Officer Dale says, "We believe a woman named Rachael is living there. We believe they kidnapped her and have her there without her permission. There is no telling what they are doing to her. She is a very troubled young woman. Her night terrors get her in lots of trouble."

Steven says, "We're on top of this. It has been a long investigation, and we will crack it soon. We just can't raid the place. If we don't get them legally, they will walk away free and clear. We have to be very careful."

Officer Dale says, "Her family is going crazy. She has been missing for quite a while. Please speed up your operation. I can help if you need it. This woman is very creative and always gets herself in trouble. She is not afraid to investigate herself, which gets her in trouble all the time. Don't forget that about her."

CHAPTER FIFTY
THE TRUTH COMES OUT

Cindy walks in my door after breakfast and says, "What's up with you, girl? Are you sick?"

"Yes … I think I'm pregnant. Damn girl, I have all the symptoms. I'm nauseated all the time, and I am throwing up every morning."

"Do you—or does anyone you know—have a pregnancy test? I hope it is not true. If it is, I'm going to kill myself."

"Oh my gosh, girl. Whose baby is it? Is it Leader Charles or Jerry's? I know both had sex with you. I bet you don't know since they took turns with you. Sorry I'm being so blunt, but I know how it happens."

"Cindy, I don't even know if I'm pregnant. It may be a stomach virus. If I'm pregnant, I don't know who the father is. Dear Jesus, it's one of those monsters."

"Well, here at the commune, there are certain things that will be done. There will be no children here … it's a rule."

"I know … just get me a test please."

"I believe we have a pregnancy test in the medical supply closet. I've got to get the key from Leader Charles or Jerry. Let me go see. I will bring it to you as soon as possible."

As she strolls out of my building, I think about the hidden room in the House of Blood and my dream last night. Will someone come and rescue me? I don't think so. I remember all the blood I saw. No one could survive losing that much blood. I guess Leader Charles killed Spencer … it sure looked like it.

Cindy walks back inside and says, "When was your last period, girl? Do you remember? I hope we don't take the test too soon. Just take this test right now so that we can find out the truth. If you're pregnant, I have to tell Leader Charles and Jerry. This can't be kept secret. I don't want to have to visit the House of Isolation again."

"You've been there? Did they torture you and brainwash you too? Tell me the truth!"

She replies, "Just go to the bathroom and take the test!"

I sit on the toilet and look at the stick in my hand. If the tiny circle turns blue, I'm pregnant. As it slowly turns blue, I start crying. Cindy is sitting on my couch. Should I tell her? I know she has to tell on me. Those monsters have gotten me pregnant.

She looks up as I walk out from the bathroom. "You're pregnant, right?"

I hand the stick to her and say, "Yes. Look at the stick. It's so blue."

"It's OK. It's only a tiny procedure, and then you will be fine."

"Have you had an abortion here before?"

"Yes. Bill got me pregnant last year, but Leader Charles took care of it for me. It didn't hurt at all. It might have hurt my feelings a little bit. Wouldn't it have been great to have a little Bill Jr. around here? You better get ready for work in the kitchen. Just grab some crackers to settle your stomach. I hope we have something good to eat tonight."

"Cindy, you're so wild—and nothing bothers you here. I'm so torn up inside. I have to tell Jerry. Please give me a few days. Don't tell Leader Charles or Jerry yet. I need to do it."

As she is walking out the door, she says, "Yes, of course, but only a few days. That means two days. If you haven't spilled the beans, then I will. I will not keep secrets for you, girl. I don't want to get in trouble for covering up something."

"Did you tell them why you needed the key to the supply room? Won't they know that something is up?"

"I told them I needed some Band-Aids for the kitchen. I've asked for them before. It's so easy to cut your finger while dicing vegetables. Just tell Jerry as soon as possible, girl. This is not something you can hide for long. I don't want to be caught in a lie."

I know the truth must come out sooner or later. I will tell Jerry after dinner tonight. After our worship time, he will be in a good mood. I will kiss him in hidden places that will make sure he is in a good mood. That is the best time to spring the bad news on him. It's not even my fault, but I will be blamed.

Dinner and worship time are so much fun. As we are walking back to our building, I know the House of Peace will not be so peaceful tonight. Jerry will be so mad at me. I hope he doesn't get violent. I don't know how to tell him, but being honest is probably the best thing. Will they put me back in that torture building?

"Jerry?"

"Yes, Rachael? You seem so quiet. Do you have something you need to talk to me about?"

As we walk into the house, I say, "I'm pregnant. I took a pregnancy test today that Cindy brought me when she went to get the Band-Aids for the kitchen."

His face turns red, and he screams, "You stupid bitch! You have been trouble since you walked into this commune. I can't believe I have a soft spot in my heart for you. Just wait until I tell Leader Charles. He will be so angry at you."

I say, "I didn't cause it. You and Leader Charles did it to me!"

Jerry slaps my face, picks me up, and carries me toward the torture house.

Here we go again.

I'm crying so hard, but nothing I say will stop Jerry. He is out of control. My mind remembers what happened there. Will this ever stop?

CHAPTER FIFTY-ONE

AND SO IT BEGINS AGAIN

I'm strapped to the cold table, and Jerry injects something into my arm. I used to be scared of needles, but I'm used to them now. Can this really be happening again? These two lowlifes are killing me with drugs and torture. Why are they torturing me when they got me pregnant? I think I might have a miscarriage and avoid having an abortion. They both are idiots.

I guess they get off on the bondage thing, and they think I deserve this punishment. I can't think of any other reason. Jerry turns on a scary movie and storms outside as I fade into a dream from hell.

Someone is chasing me, and I'm running from them. I look back, and I trip and fall. A pack of wolves is chasing me now. They are so close that I can feel their breath on the back of my neck. The ground is cold, and I feel like death is nearby. All of a sudden, a girl starts chasing the wolves. It is my little sister—my protector to the end. Veronica is so brave and strong. I'm the opposite of her; I'm such a scaredy-cat. They grab Veronica, and she starts screaming. I jump up and run to save her. Just before I reach her, they drag her away. I can see Veronica's blood dripping from their mouths. This pack of wolves is going to get both of us.

I wake up suddenly, but I don't scream. I am shaking all over, and I'm still strapped to the cold table. The weird movie is still running. I'm so miserable, and tears are flowing down my cheeks. I can't even wipe them away.

I remember my dream and my sister Veronica. Oh, what joy to know that I have a sister. I remember that I also have another one named Theresa. I hope I will be rescued from this place because I have a past that is slowly coming back to me through my dreams. As soon as I can, I will write this down in my secret notebook. Why do I dream so much about wolves chasing me? It's probably because I think Leader Charles and Jerry are wolves who are about to devour me. I'm so scared. I wonder when they will come get me.

Leader Charles storms into the room with a wild look on his face. "Rachael, are you sure you are pregnant?"

I reply weakly, "Yes, sir. I took a pregnancy test, and it was positive. I don't know who the baby's father is, but it's either you or Jerry. I'm so sorry this has happened. I love this commune and all the people here."

His face turns to complete rage. He attacks me and hits my face, my stomach, and the bottoms of my feet. I am in so much pain. Is he trying to kill the baby? He is hitting me so much in the stomach. Why does he hate children so much? I wonder if he was beaten as a child. His mind is so warped. I am going to lose this baby, but is it going to happen right now? Why do these people have such bad tempers?

He says, "You have become something horrible that has invaded our commune twice now. I have prayed and asked God to surrender you to our cause. I have done everything I know to make you change and not be a burden to our kingdom. I want to get rid of you, but that is impossible. We are not murderers here; we are saints from God. I will be back later to plan for your future here."

I have completely mixed up my days and nights. My body is hurting from the beatings, but I'm thankful to be alive. How can I get out of here alive? I don't want to be carried out in a body bag or buried in a shallow grave. Do they have shallow graves here? When I was cleaning windows with Franks, I didn't see anything that looked like a graveyard. Of course, Frank didn't let me go to certain. It will do no good to ask Frank. He really doesn't tell me that much—only to watch the woods. Heck, I don't need to do that since all my nightmares are either about the woods or the river. This place is scary. I'd really freak out if I found a graveyard here.

I drift off to sleep again.

I'm walking toward the river that is so familiar to me. There are many children swimming on floats. Everyone is so happy. They are laughing and splashing in the water. I see that weird kid, Harold, walking down to the shallow end. He is holding a mouse and a knife.

I am now standing near the shallow end too.

Harold is hitting the water over and over, and Sarah and Ryan are floating with their eyes cut out. There is blood everywhere, and it slowly dissolves in the water.

Harold turns around and sees me. He starts stabbing himself in the stomach.

I'm terrified, and I let out a bloodcurdling scream.

As I wake up from this horrendous dream, I'm still on the table. I'm shaking all over, but I don't scream. I guess my mind is getting used to the terror. Everything I've seen in my dreams happened in my life. This really did happen. I need to write it down in my secret notebook. This part of my past life is true. More and more of my past is coming out in my dreams. My nightmares have always been horrible, but maybe they will help me now. I need to make a plan to get out of this place.

When will someone come and get me off this table? I can't stand the movies and the horrific dreams any longer. I am completely sick of this place and the predicament I'm in. Please, God, help me get out of this ordeal.

CHAPTER FIFTY-TWO

BACK TO THE HOUSE OF BLOOD

Leader Charles and Jerry enter my torture building. I'm in so much pain, but I keep my eyes closed. I do not want them to know that I am awake. They are talking, and I listen carefully.

Leader Charles says, "Jerry, she's bad spiritually and physically to our commune. I don't want any of her evil ways rubbing off on our faithful followers. She is an abomination to our commune. She might even get us caught doing something that is not quite lawful. I hate all the outsiders; they point their fingers at us like we are criminals. We are just trying to make a living. I want to get rid of her once and for all."

Jerry says, "I will do anything to keep her alive. Let's just get rid of the baby and continue our process with her. I can't help it. I love this girl."

"I know you don't want her gone, but this is making me worry. She saw that woman entering our surgery house. I don't want to get in trouble with the law because of her blabbing about it. As far as anyone on the outside knows, we are just a commune full of faith and following the Lord."

"I know we don't want the laws involved, but the TV reporter and the biker gang have been the only outsiders here. The women who need our help also come in and out. They don't tell anyone because they don't want to get caught having an abortion."

"I know we won't get caught if we keep a low profile. Let's just get her over to the House of Blood and take care of business. You have made this decision, and I'm going along with it now. If she causes any more trouble, you will not get your way. She will be killed. Do you hear me, Jerry?"

"Yes, sir!"

They unstrap me, sit me up, and put a gown on me. I'm so groggy, but I try to wake up fully. They carry me over to the abortion building. I can barely walk, and I'm so unsteady on my feet. I look around to see if any of the followers are watching me. Most of them will ignore what's going on because they don't want to get in trouble. They probably already know what has happened to me. Cindy is such a blabbermouth.

I remember the blood house fully well. I lived there the last time I was here. I need to write that down too. The walls are all painted red and are so shiny. It looks like real blood is flowing down the walls. I remember sleeping here with Jerry and how cold it was on the couch. I think they also did an abortion on Cindy here. It was in one of my dreams. I need to write that down too.

I pretend that I'm very out of it and don't make a noise as they move me to the couch. I'm so glad I can walk a little bit today. I wonder if I will survive this, especially now that I will be getting an abortion. What if they use a rusty clothes hanger on me, and I get an infection? Will these people be able to save me?

Jerry says, "Leader, we can do the procedure tomorrow … first thing in the morning. She will heal here, and then I will move her back in with me. I can't believe this happened, but we can take care of it."

Leader Charles says, "That sounds like a plan to me. Now, let's go to breakfast and Morning Celebration. I need to let our followers know that we are doing just fine here. I need to keep them happy all the time and make them feel that the presence of God is here. I don't want anyone else fighting us like this filthy piece of trash."

Jerry says, "I'll send Cook in here to feed her. She needs some strength before her procedure tomorrow."

I hear the door shut as they leave.

I keep my eyes closed, but tears are rolling down my face. This is the most awful thing that I have done in my life. I have really screwed up things now. I wonder if it will hurt during the procedure. Will they give me something for the pain? They better give me an antibiotic; otherwise, I could get an infection. After this unprofessional abortion, will I be able to have any more babies? I remember that I already have two children. John and James are their names. I hope I can have another baby, maybe a girl. I need to write all of this down in my secret spiral notebook. I cannot be caught with it. I have to be careful.

Cook walks into the building and says, "You have really gotten yourself in trouble again. Can't you just keep your mouth shut and do your chores."

I reply weakly, "Cook, don't be mad at me. Are they going to hurt me?"

"I don't know. Here's your breakfast, girl. Hang in there."

Cindy walks in and seems so happy. "Frank is working already. I came to check on you. I need to tell you that the abortion won't hurt. They will give you a painkiller."

"I hope not. I'm so tired and weak. I don't know what I would do without you."

"Well, we girls have to stick together. Sometimes we get ourselves into trouble. When I first got here, I didn't understand how the commune made money to survive and pay the bills. I realized that we pretty much live by eating the food that we grow here."

"I know that, but something else has to pay the electric and water bills."

Cindy says, "Yep, and that's why Leader Charles set up a medical facility to allow women to have abortions discreetly. This place is safe, and no one on the outside finds out what they have chosen to do. It gives the commune extra money to pay for things."

"You've got to know this is illegal and not approved by medical professionals."

"What they don't know won't hurt them, right?" She walks toward the door. "You will be fine in the morning, and I will check on you after your procedure. Don't worry about this place. It is not an evil house; it's what makes us survive here."

After she leaves, I remember that I love the commune. Do I really feel this way—or is my brain so confused from all the brainwashing?

I drift off to sleep.

I am running away from someone in the woods. It is too dark to see their face, but I notice the clothes hangers in their hands. I feel the pain between my legs and the blood flowing down them. As they get closer and closer, I see Spencer and Frank watching me. Leader Charles is laughing at them as he catches me.

I wake up screaming and shaking all over. Will these nightmares ever end?

CHAPTER FIFTY-THREE
BLOODY THOUGHTS

I'm on my couch, and I hear a noise outside. I listen carefully and hear it again outside the living room window. I'm so scared. I don't want anyone to know I'm awake. I am shaking all over. Who could it be?

I wake up again and remember I'm sleeping on the couch and not that horrible table. I look around and see the bloody walls. I know it's not blood on them, but it looks like it. I close my eyes again and imagine what is about to happen to me. I listen closely, but I can't hear a thing. Who was looking in my window?

Leader Charles and Jerry open the door, and it is still dark outside. I guess it is early morning. I hear the abortion door being unlocked and talking together. I pretend to be asleep.

Leader Charles says, "I wish this would be over for all of us. You are the one who is keeping her alive. I believe she is an abomination to our commune, and God knows that her heart is evil. We haven't given others chances like this. When they are bad, they are bad."

Jerry replies, "Just give her one more chance ... please. I don't know what it is with this girl, but I'm crazy about her."

I hear them moving things around. I guess they are getting everything in order to take care of things. I'm not sad because I don't want to have a baby that comes from evil people. I hope they don't destroy my ability to have babies. I wonder if they will be nice to me and try to do a good job. I hope they don't mess me up.

Jerry picks me up, puts me on the table, and injects something in my arm. What are they always injecting into me? I feel nothing as I drift off to sleep.

I'm not sure how long the procedure takes, but I wake up in bed in his horrible building. I feel a dull pain in my lower abdomen as I drift off to sleep again.

I'm at home with Gary and my two baby boys. They are playing with their toys in their bedroom. Leader Charles is holding a bloody clothes hanger. Why is he at my house? I start shaking again. Gary sits in the floor, ignoring everyone, and starts playing with the boys. I scream as Leader Charles grabs me and ties my hands with the hangers. Gary just turns his head toward me and stares.

I wake up to Cindy shaking my shoulders. "Shut up, Rachael. You're going to wake the dead."

"Cindy, my dreams are horrible. What is said around me and done around me somehow enters my night terrors. I don't know what I'm going to do." I need to write down my last dream in my secret notebook. If I escape, I can use it against these awful people.

Cindy says, "How are you feeling? I told you it wouldn't hurt. You will be fine. Your face is a bit white, but in a few days, you will be walking around and be ready to start your chores again. Cook is on her way with some food. Eat up and get strong again. We need you doing your chores again."

"Yes, I will. It wasn't so bad. You were right. I didn't feel a thing."

As she walks toward the door, she says, "Don't screw up again, Rachael. I overheard Leader Charles and Jerry saying that this is your last chance."

Doesn't she realize that those two horrible monsters did this to me? I did nothing except lie there as they raped and beat me. When they captured me, they knew I was a bad apple. They knew they needed to make me forget my past so that I wouldn't escape and tell on them for everything they are doing.

Cook enters and doesn't even make eye contact as she places my breakfast on the table. Why doesn't she realize I'm innocent? I guess she is disgusted with me and no longer likes me. Maybe she doesn't want to get in trouble for showing me any concern. I need to do extra work in the kitchen. I need her to brag about my work so I can feel good about something. This place stinks.

As I drift off to sleep, I hear a noise outside my window. I'm still so drugged that I don't get scared. I wish they would rescue me. I hear the noise again, and it is louder this time. In my drugged state, I think a monster is coming to eat me. I think I'm about to die. My imagination is going wild. I see a zombie staring at me through the window. A corpse is looking at me and reaching out to me with the longest fingers. Its nails are long and pointed. The first zombie spawns another one. How many are out there? I'm not even scared. What is wrong with me? Why am I seeing these things? Are the drugs making me hallucinate? I guess so.

I wake up again and look toward the window, but I see nothing. Even though my stomach hurts, I walk over to the window. I look outside, but I don't see anything. I thought I was a scaredy-cat, but I can be brave at times. I guess the drugs are making me see things.

When I get out of here, I'm going to write a whole lot of stuff in my notebook. My mind has gone crazy.

I drift off to sleep again.

Someone is dead, and Leader Charles is burying them behind the House of Love. His shovel has blood all over it, and he keeps digging and digging. A man walks up and stares at the shallow grave. It's that weasel man, Ernie. Leader Charles takes out a gun and shoots him. Ernie just starts laughing. I see no wounds on Ernie as he runs away. Leader Charles sees me hiding behind a tree and tells me to come out. I am shaking all over as I step out. He points the gun at my head. I close my eyes as I hear a loud blast. I then feel nothing.

I wake up screaming, and my stomach hurts so much. I guess the drugs have worn off. What was that dream about? Is someone going to get killed here? I guess it will be me for sure. Why is it at the House of Love? When I saw the windows of that building, I thought orgies probably went on in there. Is there a graveyard behind the building? I wish I had my secret notebook here so I could write all this down. I know it was just a dream, but it feels like something bad is about to happen. Do I have premonitions?

CHAPTER FIFTY-FOUR
TRIPS TO TOWN

I am healing for a few days, and I try to remember my past. I wish someone would save me. I remember my husband, Gary, and two boys, James and John. I remember Mama, Dad, and my brother and two sisters. I remember that things are fading fast for me at the commune. If it wasn't for my horrific dreams, I would have no memories left at all. I'm writing in my spiral notebook all the time, and new things from my past are coming back to me.

Cindy arrives and says, "Girl, you won't believe this. Leader Charles and Jerry have given me permission to take you to town to pick up our medical supplies."

I reply, "Are you kidding me?"

"Nope, I talked to Frank about it, and he asked Jerry. Apparently, Jerry got an OK from Leader Charles. I was told that I must watch you like a hawk and not let you get away. I told them that you are too weak to run. I felt that it would help you mentally and physically to get away. We are just going for the medical supplies and won't be gone long."

"Cindy, you must have a lot of clout here to talk them into letting me ride with you. I'm so excited to get away. I promise I won't run away. This will be an adventure for us. We will be like Thelma and Louise! Where are we going?"

"Rachael, they have given me a gun, and if you run, I have to shoot you. Please don't run. I don't want you dead, but Leader Charles does. I think they want you to go with me to test you. If you don't prove that you can be a loyal follower, they will get rid of you—one way or the other."

This is crazy. I just had an illegal abortion, and now they are letting me go somewhere. This is awesome, but it's also scary. What if someone recognizes me? I tell myself that I will be good and make them trust me again. I can't wait to go with Cindy, and I get dressed quickly. Cindy goes to get the car. It is unbelievable that I get to go somewhere. I'm so excited that I forget the horrible abortion.

I can't dwell on the past. I have to get on with my life. There's nothing I can do. I have to get back in the good graces of these people, especially Leader Charles and Jerry. I can't wait to move back in with Jerry. If I have a bad dream, Jerry will get mad at me. Between worshipping at church and the chores, I know my mind will be healed. Doesn't the Bible say that bad company corrupts good character? Well, I won't be hanging out with bad company. I hope it means that I will be the best person I can be.

Cindy drives up, and I run over to her car. I am so excited. There will be no funny business today. I must be trusted again.

I must remember the directions in case I get to run away. So much for trying to fit in here and being happy. I'm always thinking about how to escape.

Cindy is talking her head off again.

I try to listen to her, but then I quit and start paying attention to where we are going. We have been on the road for about two hours, and I start seeing places that I've seen before. I look for any people I might know. I used to go to church here, and I had many friends. Where are they now when I need them? We are in a bad part of town. When I was growing up, Mama and Dad told me to stay away from here. They said that thieves, druggies, and criminals hung out there. I am scared, but Cindy doesn't seem fearful at all. I know she has been here before. She is used to this horrible place.

Cindy continues to chat about all kinds of things as we drive up behind a large building. The garage door is open, and I see two men in there. Cindy opens her hatchback, and they load her car with boxes. They place more boxes in the back seat. I don't recognize the men, but Cindy thanks them for the supplies. She places a white envelope in one of the men's hands. I guess they have to be paid. I have so many questions in my head. Did we just deal with two crooks?

We're on the road again, going back to the commune, and Cindy says, "If you do good, girl, you will get to go again. They like me and totally trust me. I've been here so long and have never done anything to get in trouble. If you continue to do good, and you're still Jerry's wife, they will select you again. Upper management gives their loved ones extra privileges. Keep doing good, Rachael, and you'll never have to leave. It will be your home, and you will love it just like I do."

"I know, Cindy. This is a lovely place to live. I love the worship services and the followers. I need to stop dreaming in front of anyone, especially Jerry. I know he will tell Leader Charles. I'm so scared of what he does to me. It messes with my mind." I laugh. "I will be watching movies on that table again. They seem to work very well with me. My dreams have lessened and are not as vivid as they used to be. You wouldn't believe how many I had growing up. I dreamed someone was trying to get me all the time. I heard things at night, and I thought monsters were trying to kill me. I want to forget that and not have any night terrors."

Cindy replies, "Yes, I want to live there forever. I love Frank so much. My past life is gone, but it wasn't good anyway. I'm just moving forward."

In the back of my mind, I feel like something bad is coming. Why do I still believe something horrible is going on at the commune? I know all the illegal things they do there. Didn't Cindy say they grew marijuana there? I guess they sell it too. I think about all the possibilities. Am I living with criminals? Why am I asking myself these stupid questions? Of course, they are. I've always thought that about them. They are horrible people.

CHAPTER FIFTY-FIVE
NEAR NORMAL

After we return from our road trip, we are met at the car by the followers. They start unloading Cindy's car. Everyone is staring at me, and I think they are wondering why I got to go to town. Cindy thinks it's a test to see if I can be trusted. If I make pass this test, what else will they ask me to do? I'm already picking up the medical supplies for the illegal abortions. What else will I be asked to do here?

We probably picked up illegal drugs. I know they use really strong drugs on people, especially me. I wonder if meth is used here. It would make sense that they torture people here. They are out of their minds and will do anything. What other drugs are here? I don't know since I've never done drugs. I need to write down this information in my notebook.

Leader Charles, Jerry, and Cindy go into the House of Power. I guess she is returning the gun. Cindy comes back to the car and helps unload it. They don't trust me very much if I have to be guarded with a gun. How can I be so suspicious of a place and also love it?

Cindy hands Bettye a small box. I didn't see it in Cindy's car. What is in the box? Is it drugs? Why is Bettye getting them? She is just an old woman who works in the laundry room. Maybe she is trusted here and hides them from everyone. That laundry room has many places to hide things. Maybe I can find them without getting caught. I've gotten caught too many times to think this way. Who am I fooling?

After the car is unloaded, we all go to the Morning Celebration. Leader Charles announces that we all need to be blessed by God and hear his Word. I agree with most of what Leader Charles preaches, but he sometimes says things that are not what I learned when I was growing up. Worship is good, and the followers all seem so happy. I'm still happy here, but I know there is more out there for me.

We all walk to the canteen for lunch. We are laughing and talking about how good the service was. No one talks about what we unloaded from the car. I feel joy in my heart. It was a great service. I'm a lucky girl to have been chosen to go pick up supplies. Maybe I can love it here without all the brainwashing.

Cindy says, "Rachael, you did good. This is progress. You will get to go again soon. They need to know that you can be trusted. You screwed up before and ran away. They don't want that to happen again."

"I know, but I was so upset when I saw you and Jerry in bed together. I thought I killed both of you. In my mind, I saw myself stabbing both of you with a knife. I guess it was one of my bad dreams. I had murder in my heart, but I have asked God to forgive me."

"Rachael, I'm sorry about that. It was just one time, and Jerry told me that he would never do it again. Besides, do you think little old you could kill both of us at the same time? Jerry would have beaten your ass. And then you were gone. He got so upset after you left. He was out of his mind. He wanted to go searching for you, but

Leader Charles convinced him that you would come back. It took a while, but you came back!"

"I know I'm back, and I'm very happy here."

In the back of my mind, from my dreams, I know I had a life outside of the commune. I see it in my dreams all the time. I have to be very careful not to let anyone know that I'm having visions of my past life. Do I want to go back to my old life? I'm finally fitting in again. The brainwashing and torture have lessened. Thank goodness.

I am so tired, and I go to bed. My mind is thinking about the little yellow car that we took to town to pick up supplies. Aren't they scared that someone will see it? Probably not. I hid it behind my house most of the time. Gary would recognize it, but he would not be out and about. He would be working at the school. I just remembered something—and I wasn't dreaming. I jump up and get my notebook. My memory is coming back. If they find out, I will be put through that awful brainwashing again. I will never let them know that it did not work.

I'm going to be happy here at this commune, aren't I?

I drift off to sleep.

I'm walking through each car on a train, and I'm searching for someone to save me. I see people I know, and they smile at me. I see Gary talking to a woman. I'm so jealous that I go over and tell her to get away from my man—and to never talk to him again. Someone comes over and asks me to sing for everyone. They think I'm famous. I leave with them, but I look back at the woman to make sure she is leaving my man alone. I want to kill her.

When I wake up, I wonder why I had that dream. Am I a jealous person? If I killed Cindy and Jerry, I guess I am. While I was gone the last time, Anne, our babysitter, got my man. I don't want anyone to have Gary or Jerry. It looks like I would kill for that—or at least do it in my heart. I grab my notebook and write down all this new information. Wasn't Anne a bad person?

CHAPTER FIFTY-SIX

BACK TO THE HOUSE OF PEACE

I am living with Jerry again in the House of Peace. He is making me sleep on the couch because of my night terrors. I have healed completely from the abortion and have started back to chores. I will be working in the kitchen with Cook all week. I hope she can forgive me for the problems I have caused. I will work hard for her.

Jerry says, "Good morning. I hope you didn't have bad dreams last night. I didn't hear you—thanks for that. I have a meeting with Leader Charles this morning. I will meet you at breakfast in the canteen in about an hour, OK?

I reply, "I'll be there."

He gives me a kiss and walks out the door.

I take a shower and get dressed. I'm excited about getting to work in the kitchen. I wonder why Jerry is meeting with Leader Charles. It sounds like something is going on around here. I hope I'm not getting in trouble again.

As I arrive in the canteen, Jerry is talking to Cindy. It makes me jealous, but I try to ignore it.

Jerry walks over and says, "Hi, darling. You look pretty today."

All my jealousy walks out the door, and I smile. "Good morning, Cook. I'm here to work with you this week. I feel so much better. Please tell me what you need me to do."

Cook says, "We are having sandwiches and fresh vegetables for lunch. I will show you how to make a ranch dressing with herbs and sour cream. Go ahead and start cutting the carrots, celery, cucumbers, and zucchini for the dip. Also, grab the lettuce and tomatoes for the sandwiches."

"Yes, ma'am. This will be delicious and healthy for everyone. I love the food we get to eat here. I don't see anyone getting sick, and I'm sure it's because we eat healthy food."

Cook says, "I want you to go ahead and start prepping the vegetables for dinner. You have plenty to do today, girl."

I feel very comfortable with Cook. I'm closest to Cindy, but I can talk about personal things with Cook. Cook has been bringing me food and has seen me in all kinds of predicaments. She has fed me when I couldn't even lift my head. If I ever get rescued, they should talk to her first. She has seen plenty of things here.

"Cook, am I going to survive here at the commune? I've done so many things wrong. I can't stop dreaming. They are so real and vivid, and when I wake up, I'm shaking and screaming. I get myself into so much trouble."

"Rachael, I've been here a long time, and they have been good to me. I have obeyed all the rules and haven't gotten in trouble. I don't have bad dreams like you do. That makes things easier for me. You need to work harder since you must deal with this conflict. Just try harder, and you will do fine here."

"I want to live here and make everyone happy. I love the worship services and praising God. I love Jerry. He is good to me except when I have bad dreams. I scare him and keep him from getting a good night's rest. I'm going to pray more and would like you to pray for me too. I'm so tired of the dreams, and I'm too old to be having nightmares."

Cook bows her head. "Dear God, please help Rachael to not dream anymore. We ask that you do this so that she can live here in our little heaven on earth. We know you created it for us. In Jesus's name. Amen."

I thank Cook for the prayer. I hope it helps my mind, body, and soul. I need to keep praying.

The followers start coming into the canteen for lunch. We already have it prepared and ready to put out for them. Their faces look radiant. They look so appreciative of what they have here. I need to be the same way. Not everyone gets to live in a place of love like we have here.

Jerry walks up to me and asks me to sit with him.

I reply, "I can for a little while, but then I need to get back to the kitchen to help Cook prepare dinner. I'm trying so hard to do good things and not be a burden."

"Rachael, I believe you will do the right thing. You have been through so much tribulation, but God will see you through. I really don't like myself because I've become too soft toward you. You drive me crazy with those horrible dreams."

"Jerry, tonight, after worship, I will show you how much I love you. Just wait and see."

Jerry laughs and continues eating.

I hope I can show him my love and not dream tonight. It would be so much fun to get to sleep with him the whole night.

As Jerry is walking out the door, he says, "Rachael, I can't wait until tonight!"

I return to the kitchen and work with Cook until dinnertime.

Jerry and I go to Worship Night. Everyone is singing and praising. I lift my hands in thanks for being alive and getting to live here. The followers all seem so happy to be living here too. I'm sure they all are glad to have a place to live. Their prior lives must have been horrible. I know we all make mistakes and put ourselves in situations that we can't crawl out of. I figured they all hit rock bottom with drinking and drugs. When you hit rock bottom, sometimes this is where you show up—with no place to go. We all get here on the same train. No one is better than the other.

After loving on Jerry for a long time, I hear him doze off. I go to the couch. I cannot risk having another bad dream around Jerry. I didn't want to wake him and make things worse for me. I'm in such a good mood and feel so good as I drift off to sleep.

I see Leader Charles and Jerry, and they are whispering about a dead man. If they are whispering, how can I know what they are saying? I walk toward them and see a man on the ground. He is dressed in a very odd outfit. It looks as though he has a red shirt on, but I realize it is blood. His eyes have been cut out and placed on the ground beside him. What? He looks like someone I have seen before. Is he the cowboy from my childhood dreams? His face looks like a clown's face, and there is a large red nose in the middle. I think he is dead, but then he starts smiling at me. I am very frightened. His eyes are gone, and his incredibly large lips are smiling at me. I see rats running all around him and eating his flesh, and I take a step back. I fall into a bloody river. Why is the water so red? As I am thrashing in the water, almost unable to keep my head above the water, I remember that I don't want to drown. I want to live. I see the dead man floating past me. I guess Leader Charles and Jerry threw him in the river.

I wake up shaking with goose bumps on my arms. I remember my dream distinctly. Who was that dead man? I still have my horrible dreams, but now they do not disturb me so badly. After the brainwashing and horrible beatings, nothing bothers me. Maybe I can sleep with Jerry all night now.

CHAPTER FIFTY-SEVEN
COME FIND ME

Officer Dale arrives in Laredo to assist in the investigation of locating Rachael and bringing down the commune. The Laredo police find out that a man named Ernie has moved to the commune. The authorities know that the commune is aware of them being watched. They are afraid that the leaders in the commune are trying to build up an army to fight the police. Not all communes are bad, and some are safe havens for people. This commune, however, is doing unlawful things.

Frank has been able to communicate with the outside via a phone that is hidden in the woods. He is such a good investigator that he is able to slip around without being caught. Frank used to be a marine and was trained to get in and out of places without being seen. He is a professional, and he will be able to bring down the commune.

Frank lets the police know about Ernie and how he has sent many types of guns into the commune. Frank is informed that

Officer Dale is there. The police tell Frank that they will investigate Ernie and let him know what type of criminal he is. Frank is worried that he is a professional gunman and will defend the commune with Leader Charles, Jerry, and their men. When Ernie arrives at the commune, Frank will be waiting for him.

Frank tells the police all about the leaders and the other people at the commune. He tells them that illegal drugs being purchased and sold there. Marijuana is being grown and sold, and illegal abortions are being performed. The followers are being tortured and brainwashed, and there is a graveyard behind the community building. There are many graves, and a new one is being dug. He doesn't know who it is for, and he hasn't heard any news about it from Leader Charles or Jerry. They are being very secretive and are keeping Frank out of the loop.

The authorities do not want a shoot-out at the commune. Many innocent people live there. They are only there for a roof over their heads. Some of the followers have shady pasts and will defend the commune. Frank wants to find out where the weapons are being hidden. Before anything happens, they must take out the commune's defensive weapons.

Frank tells Rachael to stay safe and watch for people in the woods. He wants her to be prepared for anything. He's not sure how much she understands since she has been brainwashed. He's not sure if she remembers her past.

The police ask Frank to let them know when it is safe to go in. They want to have enough information to shut down the commune. They don't want another murder to happen there.

CHAPTER FIFTY-EIGHT

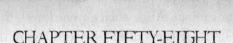

NIGHTLY INVESTIGATIONS

After a long day working with Cook, I enjoy the Worship Night with Jerry and my friends. I notice Leader Charles and Jerry whispering and wonder what is going on. As I worship and give thanks for my life, I decide that I need to pay more attention to what is going on here. I need to find out if criminals are running this place.

Even after all the brainwashing and torture, I still remember some of my past. I do have a past, and I need to find out more about it. Is this commune all there is out there? Do I have a better life on the outside? I need to review what I've written down to keep my memory in check. My mind fades so quickly.

I need to find out what is going on between Leader Charles and Jerry, and I need to find out more about Frank. He has said some very confusing things to me. Is Frank one of them? Are they making plans to harm me or kill me?

After our lovemaking, Jerry starts to snore. When he is fully asleep, I put on my sneakers and go out to the bushes in front of our building. I don't want anyone to see me. If I'm caught, there's no telling what will happen to me. I'm not going to get caught this time. I will be so careful that I won't even hear myself.

Leader Charles and Frank are talking outside the chapel. Have they been talking since worship ended? I crawl past the bushes and stop behind a large tree. So far, they haven't looked up. I hear pieces of their conversation, and I hope they don't hear my heart beating out of my chest.

Frank says, "Leader Charles, we must be careful about who comes into our campus. Also, when anyone leaves, they need to be very careful. If Cindy gets pulled over with a gun, the police will arrest both of them. There are people out there who don't want us to be doing good. They are trying to catch us doing bad things."

Leader Charles replies, "I know. I only sent a gun with Cindy because she had our troublemaker with her."

Frank asks, "Why was she on that trip? Wasn't that risky?"

Leader Charles replies, "It was very risky, but I needed to know if Rachael could be trusted on the outside. I don't believe I will let her go again. That was a last-minute decision I made, just hoping she doesn't have to die."

Frank says, "I don't want her to die either. Jerry doesn't want her dead, and you know that. On the next road trip, I would like to go with Cindy. She is my wife, and we trust each other the most. We know you trust us both too. We have earned that here. What do you think?"

Leader Charles replies, "Yes, you can go. There will be a run for medical supplies on Thursday. You and Cindy can go. Just go straight there and back. No sidetracking or silly business."

Frank says, "Yes, sir. Can we talk about the guy who helps us with the lie detector equipment? Isn't he from San Antonio?"

Leader Charles says, "Why are you asking about him?"

Frank says, "Well, Jerry mentioned him to me, and I was just wondering if he could be spying on us. Do you know if he keeps his mouth shut? I think we need to pay him a visit just to make sure."

Leader Charles replies, "For as much money as he costs, he better keep his mouth shut. He stole that equipment. He is a crook and if he comes around here or goes blabbing his mouth about us, he will be history. He might be able to help us."

Frank says, "I don't think he will come around here, but I do think he might rat us out. We don't want the authorities to find out anything that is going on here."

Leader Charles says, "If you are talking about that stranger who came here, I took care of him. He was a thief, and he was going to rob us. The only people who need to come into this compound are women who need things taken care of. That biker gang should not have found us, but they did."

Franks asks, "Where did you bury him? I hope someplace where no one can find the body."

Leader Charles says, "It's taken care of, Frank. If I need your help disposing of a body, I'll let you know."

Frank starts walking away, but he turns around and says, "One last thing … on Thursday, do we need to take a gun?"

Leader Charles replies, "No, I don't want to risk that."

My feet and legs are numb. I have heard a lot tonight. I wonder if they buried the dead man in a grave in the woods or threw him in the river. In my dream, there was a dead man in the woods and in the river. I crawl back to Jerry's building and fall asleep on the couch.

Cindy is standing beside her famous yellow car. Frank is running toward her and yelling for her to get in the car. Cindy is laughing as she falls to the ground. She has been shot and has blood all over her chest. Her beautiful psychedelic dress is all ruined now. She stops moving, and Frank grabs her and starts crying. A roach comes out of her mouth, and I wonder if she is dead.

The lie detector man comes over to Cindy's bloody body and stares at her. Her eyes are bulging, and the blood is congealing on the ground. It looks like red Jell-O. Her face is never going to be beautiful again.

Frank grabs a gun and shoots the weasel man in the face. As he is falling to the cold ground, I remember that the man's name is Ernie. He is a weasel! Blood is dripping from Cindy's body and from the man's body. Frank lifts him up and throws him into the air. It looks like he is a puppet. Ernie is floating down the river. There is blood all over the ground and in the water.

When I wake up, I'm shaking—but no screams come out of me. My dreams are so odd now. Have I gone into a stage of having these types of dreams now? Everyone is getting killed.

I then remember that Cindy and Frank are going to get supplies on Thursday. I hope they will be careful and that no one gets shot. I need to start investigating every night to find out what is really going on here. I've been brainwashed enough to love this place, but I also can't forget that I have a better life out there. I need to escape again, but I've got to figure out how to do it.

CHAPTER FIFTY-NINE
NIGHTLY RITUALS

My days are becoming more normal, and my dreams are slowing down. I'm not screaming after horrendous ones. That's odd for me, but nothing can really scare me now. I go to breakfast, and then we have the Morning Celebration sermon. We do our chores—wherever we are assigned—and then it is dinnertime and evening worship. I'm still living in the building with Jerry, and our relationship is growing. We are getting so close. I know Jerry loves me, but I also know he will turn on me in a New York minute if I dream or do something stupid.

Each night, I go to bed with Jerry, and then I sleep on the couch— even though I haven't screamed in a long time. I don't want to screw up and make him mad at me. I put on my sneakers and put pillows under my covers to make it look like I'm sleeping. I go outside and listen. I've got to figure out what is going on here and how I might be able to escape. If I'm caught, I'm a dead person. Leader Charles will not give me a second chance. I know they are capable of murder here. I don't want to die, but I've got to find out what is going on.

I have a better place to hide now. I have a secret place under a willow tree where nobody can see me or hear me. There are so many branches, and the leaves touch the ground. I can sit, in secret, without anyone seeing me. How did I get so brave?

Leader Charles and Jerry are talking. How did Jerry get out of his bedroom and go outside without me hearing him? I thought I heard him sleeping. Why didn't I hear him? Is there a secret door that I don't know about that Jerry can sneak out of? I sit very still and listen to their conversation.

Leader Charles says, "Jerry, we need to be very careful. I think we are being watched."

Jerry asks, "By who?"

Leader Charles says, "I think the feds are after us. I have spoken to a few confidants on the outside. I trust what they tell me. They could get us for murders, illegal abortions, and drug sales—just to name a few things. Hell, they could get both of us for rapes, beatings, and brainwashing."

Jerry says, "Well, we may have to disband and go someplace else. Frank and Cindy are going to make a run on Thursday for medical supplies and the other stuff. We need to tell them to be very careful."

Leader Charles replies, "Yes, for sure. If they see anyone acting suspicious or anything, they need to turn around and come back here. I don't care if they don't get the drugs—we just can't be caught."

Jerry says, "We have that man who will help us if we need him."

Leader Charles says, "Yes, you're right. I will call him. I'm ready to go to bed now. I have that sweet thing Miranda meeting me tonight. She's my favorite follower, and she doesn't mind the extra benefits I receive from her. She's a bit young, but she's so fine."

Jerry laughs. "I hear you. it's not so bad with Rachael in my bed. She keeps me satisfied … if you know what I mean."

I sure hope Jerry doesn't try to wake me on the couch. I'll be a dead person for sure.

CHAPTER SIXTY
FEAR ESCAPES ME

As I crawl back onto the couch, I give thanks to God for allowing me to not get caught. I need to keep being careful while I'm investigating at night. Maybe I should lie low for a while just to be safe. As I drift off to sleep, my nightmares return.

I'm running toward Cindy's yellow car, which is parked under the old willow tree. I realize that it's one of the trees that I hide under to do my snooping. As I jump in, I look over and see Spencer in the driver's seat. What is he doing here? He opens his mouth and smiles at me. His teeth look like eyeteeth, and blood is dripping from them. I finally have figured out who he really is. He is a vampire, and he will soon bite me and suck out all my blood. I grab my knife and start slicing his arms. He laughs at me. It looks like he feels no pain. His eyes turn bloodred. I see mice on the floorboard. Half of them are dead, and their tongues are hanging out. The other ones start biting my ankles, making them bleed. All the blood excites Spencer. He grabs my knife and slices my hand. I look down at all the blood and start laughing. This draws his attention back to me. He turns his head all around so that he can face me. He is grinning as he takes the knife and slices my throat. What? I feel no pain.

I wake up and think about this dream. I'm not shaking at all, and most of my anxiety is gone. Where has my fear gone? Why am I seeing Spencer in my dream? I remember that Spencer was my therapist at home. I was seeing him because I needed to work through the childhood nightmares that have followed me to adulthood. I told him about witnessing Harold killing my two childhood friends and escaping from him. I also needed to work through some rough times with escaping from this commune. The only thing I hadn't brought to light was that I didn't know if I had killed Jerry and Cindy.

I guess dreaming about Spencer is in my mind. I've proven that I dream about whatever I'm around or what I talk about or listen to. I don't know where he fits into all this. Is he a good guy or a bad guy? I get out my spiral notebook and start making notes about all this information from my past.

I believe the brainwashing treatments have lessened my night terrors. I'm not reacting to them with so much fear. The screaming is gone after my nightmares and weird dreams. I pray to God that this is permanent. Will I finally be able to lead a normal life without scaring everyone in my life?

My day starts with breakfast and morning worship service. This week, I am working in the garden. Since Jerry is there, I will get to see him more often. It's hot outside, but I don't mind the heat. I love weeding and picking vegetables for our meals. They are so fresh, and

I think that eating healthy is keeping us all well. I had an abortion with no complications, and my body healed quickly.

After chores, everyone cleans up and meets in the canteen.

Leader Charles announces that there will be a special speaker at our service tonight.

I say, "Jerry, do you know our speaker tonight?"

Jerry says, "Yes, he is a friend. You may remember him. That's all I'm going to say about it. You'll find out when you get there."

To my amazement, it's the guy who did my lie detector test. His name is Ernie, and I dreamed about him the other night. You have got to be kidding me. He's going to give a religious speech? How in the world did he get here?

He talks about loving God and the reasons we are here at the commune. He told us that we are commanded to love one another.

This weasel man is a crook. Leader Charles has lost his mind. I'm not his judge, but God said, "Vengeance is mine." My heart tells me that, but my mind is thinking bad things about him. I want to jump up and declare him a false prophet. If I do, I will be in major trouble. I still can't figure out why he is here.

As we are walking out of the chapel, we all have to shake hands with Ernie. I'm dreading this. I know he will recognize me. He shakes my hand and smiles at me. It is weird that he doesn't acknowledge me. I guess he doesn't want me to remember him.

Jerry grabs my hand, and we walk to our building. "Rachael, forget that you met this man before. He is not a bad man like I know you are thinking. He is here to help."

"I know, Jerry, but it's unbelievable that he showed up here. He lives a long way from here, right?"

Jerry replies, "Don't ask questions, Rachael. That will be better for you. The less you know, the better off you will be."

We make love again, and Jerry accidentally calls me Cindy. I try to ignore this, but it hurts my feelings. Is he in love with her? I thought they only had that one episode when I caught them. I'm so jealous of everyone. "Why did you call me Cindy?"

"I don't know. I guess because she is going to town this week, and that was on my mind. Don't worry, honey. You are my one and only."

I get up after a while, and I can hear Jerry's heavy snoring. I go quietly and get my spiral notebook. I need to write down some things about Cindy and Jerry. What's going on with them? I don't believe Jerry. I think he secretly still has a thing for her. For heaven's sake, they were making love in our bed! Or was it just sex with no meaning other than bodily pleasure?

CHAPTER SIXTY-ONE

FRANK AND CINDY GO TO TOWN

On Thursday, I watch Frank and Cindy leave the commune in her small yellow car. I hope they get caught and tell the authorities where I am. If they go back to my small town to pick up the medical supplies, someone will see her yellow car. I usually hid it behind my house, but Gary and my dad know about it. Mama saw it too. Maybe someone will see it and report it to the police.

I worry about getting caught breaking any of the rules. I don't want any more torture or beatings. My memory is still so vague from the brainwashing. I follow all the rules as I go to the garden, but I am still sneaking out at night to investigate.

Leader Charles is talking to Miranda. They are whispering and laughing like lovebirds. I guess they had a good night. If only she knew what he is capable of doing. She better not cross him.

Jerry is helping me weed the corn. They don't want one weed growing in them. I must not have the worst job out here. Some of the followers have coffee cans with some gas in them. They pick the bugs off the potato plants and put them in the can. Now that's a bad job to have.

Jerry stops helping me and walks over to Leader Charles. They look nervous.

Jerry says, "I can't wait until they return. I have a bad feeling when anyone goes to town. I hope no one is watching us."

Leader Charles says, "Me too. That's why we have Ernie here now. He can protect our commune from outsiders. He doesn't mind taking care of someone if they get too close. He brought many guns for us. No one is going to take us down. I will build an army if I have to."

Jerry replies, "Yes, I feel better with him here. Between all of us guys, we can hold off any attacks from the outside. If they know what is good for them, they will leave us alone."

They are both looking at me. I guess they realize I am listening to every word they are saying. I bow my head down and keep pulling weeds. I don't want to be caught listening to the leaders.

Leader Charles looks up and whispers, "She's listening. Tell her to stop getting into our business. I will take care of her. There's Cindy and Frank now. Everything is going to be all right. Let's go unpack the car."

As Jerry and Leader Charles walk away, I have an awful feeling that something evil is coming. What is it?

Jerry asks, "Did everything go OK, Frank? Was anyone suspicious watching you?"

Frank replies, "Nope, I didn't see anything. We went to the supply building, and two men helped load our car. Cindy gave them the envelope, and then we left."

Leader Charles says, "I'm glad. I was a bit nervous about who is watching us."

Frank replies, "I didn't see anyone suspicious."

A bunch of the followers unpack the yellow car, but I stay in the garden and continue weeding. I don't want to get in trouble for not helping, but I don't want to make them think I'm getting too close to what they are doing. I'm going to keep my nose clean. The punishment is too rough.

Jerry walks over to me and says, "Rachael, it's time to get cleaned up for dinner. You need to quit listening to us when we are talking. You will get in trouble, girl."

I reply, "I know, but I will do better. I don't want anyone to think I'm a spy. I love this commune, and the people are so good to me. This is my happy place, Jerry, and I'm never leaving. Please believe that."

Jerry smiles at me.

Dinner and worship are awesome tonight. I enjoy it so much. Something has put me in such a good mood. I wonder if they put something in my drink. I haven't felt this high in my life. Cindy probably drugged me because she loves it when I laugh and have fun. Jerry is enjoying my laughter too. At worship, we raise our hands and dance up and down the aisles.

Leader Charles goes to the podium and says, "My dear worshippers, we have been blessed so much here in this commune. There is no one who can take that away from us. There may be a day that comes soon when we need your help. We may need you to become defenders for us and God. If the outsiders come, we have to fight them. They are coming to steal our joy. We must fight."

All the people say, "Amen!"

I wonder what we will be asked to do. What war is coming here? Is someone going to break into the commune and steal everything? I have all these questions in my mind, but I really don't care because I'm higher than a kite. I'm going to jump Jerry's bones as soon as we get to our building. He will be so happy with me. Who drugged me?

CHAPTER SIXTY-TWO
EVIL TO COME

After an aggressive lovemaking session with Jerry, I go to the couch. I hope Jerry is sleeping. I have worn him out. I think about Gary. I made love to him too. I know this because we have two boys. I don't remember many details of my past life, and that makes me sad.

I sneak out and hide under the willow tree. I hear screams coming from the House of Power. I believe it is Miranda. I wonder if Leader Charles is raping and beating her. She is just a child—no older than sixteen. She is a runaway who escaped from her foster home. Cindy asked Miranda why she was here, and then she told me everything she said. What is going on in that awful building?

I crawl over to the building and look in the window.

Leader Charles is yelling at her. He is telling her that she is a bad girl who deserves this punishment. I hear the belt slapping her. It also hit the walls and the floor. I guess he is trying to scare her. I wonder what she did to make him so mad. Did she try to run away? How did I get so brave?

Her screams lessen, and the light goes off. I guess they are going to bed now. I crawl back to the willow tree and hide again carefully. I hope no one sees me. I need to check on her tomorrow to see if she needs to be doctored. I still have salve that I can put on her. I know how it feels to be hit like that. It will take her a while to heal.

I watch for a little longer and notice a large man walking in the dark. He is dressed all in black. Is that the cowboy from my dreams? I stare closely to try to figure out who it is, and I realize it is Frank. What is he doing out after dark? Is he up to no good—or is he guarding this place? I stay quiet as he passes by. I wait for a long time before I go back to my building. I'm so glad that Jerry is a heavy sleeper. The only thing that wakes him is when I scream from a horrible bloody dream. I make sure I don't do that any longer.

On my couch, I think about Leader Charles. He is such an evil man, and there's no telling what evil is to come here. I do not believe he is a man of God. He is a man who is using people for his own good. It gives him the power that he is seeking. I wonder how many people he has raped and beaten. I wonder who he has killed. I'm so scared of him, and I am careful to stay out his sight if possible.

What is Frank doing? If he's not careful, they will catch him. If Leader Charles isn't careful, he will be caught too. He is a bad man, and someone needs to expose him.

I drift off to sleep.

I'm so scared that I can hardly breathe. I'm running as fast as I can. Someone is chasing me in the dark. As he gets closer, I feel his breath on my neck. I stumble and look up. Leader Charles is laughing at me and showing his large green teeth. He tells me that I am going to die here. I look over, and I see Frank. He is dressed like my cowboy, and he is holding a gun. I think Frank will save me, but all he is doing is staring at us. It's as if we are zombies and have put him in a trance.

Why isn't he helping me? All of a sudden, Cindy walks over to me with a baby in her arms. The baby looks happy. Where did this baby come from? There are no babies at this commune. Leader Charles pushes me down to the ground and tells me that I have no babies. I look down, and there are two baby boys in my arms. I laugh at him and tell him to go away.

When I wake up, I remember my two babies—and I remember their names. Gary and I named them John and James. I do have babies! I quietly step into the kitchen and grab my spiral notebook, write in it quickly, and put it back in my hiding place.

I drift off to sleep again and awaken when someone starts pounding on our door. Jerry walks quickly over to answer it. It's Frank—not the cowboy. He tells Jerry that Leader Charles wants a meeting in the morning. Something has happened.

CHAPTER SIXTY-THREE
HELPING MIRANDA

It's a new day in the commune. I thank the good Lord that I'm still alive. I think about Miranda. I know she needs my help today. I know she will have whip marks up and down her back. I know she will be bleeding between her legs. I can feel her pain. I wonder if that is how Cindy feels when she knows I've gotten into trouble again.

I then notice Jerry in our kitchen. He is making himself a to-go coffee.

"Good morning, Jerry. Did you sleep well?"

"Yes, I had a good night. I didn't hear you dreaming. Is that going better?"

"I guess so. Aren't you going to breakfast with me?"

"No, we have a few situations going on, and there's going to be a meeting this morning with some of the leaders. Don't ask me what it is about because I will not tell you. There are some things that can't be shared with people we don't trust. You're doing better, but you're not completely trustworthy. I'll see you at lunch."

I think Leader Charles knows that his little wonderful world here may come crashing down soon if he is not careful. There are more men here than normal. Ernie is capable of doing bad things to people. They have him here for a reason. I wonder if Leader Charles has a crew of bad thugs that he can call when needed. I bet he does.

Before breakfast, I sneak over to the House of Power. Hopefully, Leader Charles has already gone to the meeting. I knock lightly and hear Miranda moaning. I go inside, and she is on the floor. As I thought, she has been badly beaten, and blood is running from between her legs. I help her to the couch and run to the bathroom to get a warm washrag. I run warm water into a large Tupperware bowl. I start cleaning her and put salve on the bad places. He must have used a whip on her. She is moaning and crying and going in and out of consciousness. Leader Charles is evil. How can he do this to a helpless girl? I thought this was a good place, which they lead people to believe, but it is not. Where has all the love gone?

"Miranda, you will be fine. You will heal quickly, and then you'll be able to return to your chores. You have to follow the rules around here."

"Rachael, I don't have a home. I ran away from this foster home because it wasn't good there either. I was raped there by the foster father. He is another evil man. Please help me get out of here."

"There's no getting out. You must obey the rules. Believe me, I had to find out the hard way—just like you. You will heal eventually. You will be sore for quite a while, but then you will be fine. Remember to pray every night that this will never happen again. Prayer is the only thing you have at this point. No one here is on your side. You will be fine."

"I think I am dying. How bad am I bleeding? He shoved hard cold things into me that hurt all the way to my core. He screamed horrible things at me. I just hurt so badly. Am I going to die?"

"No, you will heal and not die, girl. What did you do to make Leader Charles so mad?"

"I told him I had a boyfriend back at home and that I wanted to leave. I told him I didn't want to make love with him any longer. He flew into a rage and started beating me. It was so bad."

"I know. The same thing happened to me. Did Leader Charles know your boyfriend—or was he just jealous?"

"I could tell that he knew the guy I used to see. He asked me for a name, but I didn't tell him. He just flew into a rage."

"You will heal, but you won't forget your beating. I will be back to help you if I can. Keep this salve and put it on your wounds. I've left some pads to put between your legs until the bleeding stops. I've got to go before I get caught in here."

As I close the door, I have all kinds of bad memories of this place. In fact, this whole commune has become so wicked. The only place of peace is in the kitchen and at church. Hopefully, they will stay in my comfort zone. Will someone come and rescue us? Why are the men meeting? Are they worried about the authorities raiding this place. What have they heard? Who is the boyfriend that Leader Charles is so upset about?

After breakfast, I go to the garden to work. None of the men have shown up yet. I guess they are still meeting. As I'm working, I decide that I have to take a chance and investigate again tonight. What's going on around here? I know about the guns. I know about the rapes and beatings. I know about the brainwashing and asphyxiation. I know about the illegal abortions and the drugs.

This is not a good commune. There are evil things going on. They are all illegal, right? Will I ever get to go back to my old life? I only remember bits and pieces of it because of my dreams, but my dreams have slowed down. I'm thankful for this. I don't want to make anyone mad at me again. I want to dream and have some useful visions of my past.

I go to the canteen for lunch. The men are eating together.

Jerry waves and comes over to me.

I get my food, and we sit down with Frank and Cindy.

Everything seems normal, but I have a pit in my stomach. "Cindy, do you have any of that 'happy' medicine that you gave me the other day. I know you put it in my drink or something. Miranda needs some. She feels really bad. Leader Charles got to her too. Those rapes and beatings are awful, and she has whip marks all over her back. I know she will heal, but she is going out of her mind. If she tries to run, it will be worse for her."

Cindy whispers, "Yes, I'll slip you some before we go to our chores. Be quiet before we get caught."

Frank asks, "What are you two girls whispering about? Are you talking about your stud men? We keep you satisfied at night, don't we?"

I reply, "Please don't talk about stuff like this in public. It's embarrassing."

Cindy laughs and says, "I'm not embarrassed at all. It's so much fun!"

Miranda must be feeling horrible. Time will heal her physically and mentally. She just needs to keep all the rules. She needs to keep her mouth shut about her old life. She ran away from it. Why is she talking about old boyfriends? It must have not been as bad as she thought at the time. I need to bring her the happy medicine, and I need to make sure she knows to keep her mouth shut. She must not talk about her old life. They don't like that around here.

As Jerry and I are getting dressed for dinner and worship, I think about Miranda. I have to find a time to bring her the medicine.

Right before worship, I slip over to Miranda and give her the medicine. "Miranda, what is your boyfriend's name?"

"Spencer … why does everyone want to know his name? Is he in trouble?"

"I used to know a guy named Spencer. He looks like a nerd. Is that him?"

"Yes, and he is a good person to talk to. I used to go see him to talk, and then we started sleeping together. I eventually ran from my foster family; they were the evilest people, and they also beat me. How come I can't stay away from people who beat me?"

I can't believe she knows Spencer. Is he one of the criminals? It is incredible that we both know this guy.

I run to the chapel to meet Jerry and the other followers. I have so much to think about.

Leader Charles tells us to be ready if the outsiders come. He preaches about the prodigal son again, and I wonder if he is talking about me again.

CHAPTER SIXTY-FOUR
PREPARATION

With the men meeting all the time, I know that something is up. Are we about to be attacked by outsiders? With all the guns in this commune, the men will be able to fend off an army. Leader Charles said there will be a holy war if anyone tries to invade. I think someone will get hurt here if they are not careful.

I go about my business and do my chores, but I am constantly watching everyone and listening to what they are saying. Frank is always in the middle of things. Leader Charles and Jerry respect him a lot and let him speak his mind. From the garden, I notice that they have someone in the torture box. One of the men is guarding the door. I wonder who is in there. Who have they captured?

Jerry comes over and tells me to go to lunch with him.

As we walk by the building, I hear moans. "Jerry, who is in there?"

"Shut up, Rachael. You are so nosy, and it's best if you don't know."

"I know, and I won't say anything—just like all the other followers. No one wants to get in trouble around here. I can't wait for Worship Night tonight. I love all the praise."

After lunch, I go back to my chores and try to ignore my curiosity. I always get in trouble when I investigate, and I can't find out who is in the box because it is being guarded. I don't hear any more sounds from the box. I wonder if they died.

I meet Jerry back at our house. As we get dressed for dinner, Jerry says, "Rachael, you need to stay out of things. We are preparing for a possible invasion. I shouldn't even tell you, but I know you are so nosy."

"What are you going to do?"

"We don't know yet, but you have to stay out of it. If I hear or see you being nosy, I will beat you again. Do you hear me?"

"Yes, I promise to stay out of things. I hope no one gets hurt."

"Keep your mouth shut, Rachael. Do you hear me?"

"Yes, I hear you."

We walk over to the canteen and meet Leader Charles and Frank.

Frank says, "We are ready, Jerry."

Ready for what? Are they expecting something to happen soon?

I walk over to Cindy her and say, "Are you ready?"

"Ready for what?"

"Ready for dinner and church!"

She smiles as we line up to say grace. Frank says the prayer, but he sounds odd. It sounds like he is not used to praying. Is he a newcomer to faith? In the last part of his prayer, he says he hopes the Lord will save us. I'm already saved—isn't he?

We all sit down, and then the men go outside. What is going on here? Cindy sits there like nothing is going on.

"Cindy, aren't you scared? Are the outsiders here?"

"Shut up, Rachael. We must be quiet. Let's slip out the back door and hide in the garden. Maybe no one will find us."

I'm shaking all over, but I follow her quietly. What is about to happen?

If it is the authorities, I sure hope my brother and Officer Dale rescue us. They have probably been involved in investigating this place.

CHAPTER SIXTY-FIVE

THE RESCUE

As we are sitting in the corn, Cindy and I hear all types of shooting and yelling. We are so scared. Cindy keeps telling me to be quiet. I'm shaking all over. I hope no one finds us.

Just as things are getting quiet, someone yells, "Drop your guns!"

I hurriedly get to my feet. The commune is being raided.

Miranda is yelling, and Frank is helping her. They both have guns. They are arresting Leader Charles and Jerry. All the followers are told to sit on the ground. No one has any guns to fend off the outsiders. I'm sitting on the ground and taking it all in. They put both of these horrible men in a cop car.

Cindy runs over to them, and they hand her a gun. Police officers are everywhere.

Ernie, the weasel man, runs out of the House of Blood and fires his gun. Cindy shoots him in the forehead. I close my eyes as he hits the ground. Cindy is a cop—and a good shot too. Wow, she's a good cop too. She's been at the commune for so long. I'm so proud of her. She has saved the day.

Cindy and Miranda walk over to the torture box and open the door. Spencer is on the floor. He tries to walk, but he is weak and can hardly see. He has several cuts and bruises. I smile at him even though I know he really can't see me. I guess he was a good guy after all.

I see Joe and Officer Dale, and I run over to my brother and hug him tightly. I've been shaking since Ernie was shot. I'm glad no one else had to be killed. How did the authorities find us? I guess that is a long story.

Joe says, "Rachael, you did it again. You got yourself into big trouble here. Why do you always have to be so nosy? We had this nipped in the bud. We were going to catch these guys without your help, right?"

Officer Dale walks up and says, "I don't know about that. Thanks to Rachael and our trusty law enforcement on the inside, we have captured some really bad criminals."

I smile.

Spencer, Miranda, Frank, and Cindy were all involved in taking down that terrible place. They all worked for the Laredo Police Department. When Cindy and Frank went to town, they met with the authorities and made arrangements for the raid. It really wasn't a happy place after all.

A bus arrives, and the police officers start loading the followers. I suspect they will find out if any of them are criminals. If they are good people, we will need to help them. Maybe they can come to our little town and start a place for troubled people. Everyone needs some help from time to time.

CHAPTER SIXTY-SIX
MY GARY

I see Gary getting out of a police car. I stare at him in disbelief. I cannot believe he is in front of me. Is this real? As I walk slowly toward him, I feel pure joy. He is smiling from ear to ear, and he starts walking toward me. He has the biggest grin on his face. I start running, and he grabs me and throws his arms around me. He is holding me so tightly, and tears of joy are running down my face again.

He says, "Rachael, you are my girl!"

Printed in the United States
by Baker & Taylor Publisher Services